Tales from the Weighing Room

John Buckingham

TALES FROM THE WEIGHING ROOM

A Life in Racing

PELHAM BOOKS

First published in Great Britain by
Pelham Books Ltd
27 Wrights Lane
London W8 5TZ
1987

British Library Cataloguing in Publication Data

Buckingham, John
Tales from the weighing room.
1. Steeplechasing——Anecdotes, facetiae, satire, etc.
I. Title
798.4′5   SF359

ISBN 0-7207-1748-5

Typeset by Goodfellow and Egan, Cambridge
Printed by Butler and Tanner, England

For Ann, Laura and Lucy

CONTENTS

Photo Credits

The author and publishers are grateful to the following for permission to reproduce copyright photographs in this book: Beds and Bucks page 35; Kenneth Bright page 111; Central Press Photos pages 22, 31; Gerry Cranham pages ix, 69, 77, 113 (top and bottom); Express Newspapers pages 24/25; J. Findlay Davidson page 10 (top); Fotonews Racing Picture Service page 13 (top and bottom); Fox Photos page 37; John Grant pages 41, 46 (top and bottom); Alan Johnson pages 58, 62, 63, 107, 123; Frank H. Meads pages 40, 45 (top), 50, 90, 97, 98, 100; *News of the World* page 52; Bernard Parkin page 12; the Press Association pages 27, 28, 32; the Sport and General Press Agency pages 10 (bottom), 11, 39, 42; A.G. Templeton page 119; Douglas Weaver page 14; *Western Morning News* page 5. In some cases it has not been possible to ascertain the copyright holder and it is hoped that any such omissions will be excused.

FOREWORD

by David Nicholson

Having glibly said 'Yes, I'd love to,' when asked to write a foreword to Buck's book, I discovered that it is more difficult than I ever imagined to actually sit down and put your ideas on paper. I am not in any way a man of the written word, as John well knows, finding the telephone a much simpler instrument than a pen, but I am very honoured that he asked me to do it.

It is a long time since we were both schooling and riding the Courage horses, but it was then that I really began to get to know John, probably nicking his rides at the same time! It struck me then that here was a genuine sort of guy, whom you seldom heard complain if he was stood down in favour of a more senior or in-form jockey. However, you could never accuse him of being down-trodden — probably the reverse in fact, bouncing back to plot some dastardly weighing room prank.

When he won the Grand National, I was riding the second favourite, Bassnet, who fell at the first fence alongside the eventual trouble-maker, Popham Down. Luckily I was able to hold on to my horse, jump back on, and be back at the winning post to congratulate John in his great moment of glory. It was a tremendously deter-mined feat of horsemanship, especially as the old horse, Foinavon, was noted for being pretty idle when in front for too long.

Moving on to the cricket scene, Buck may not have been the star player of the National Hunt jockeys' team, but there was never a dull moment when he was involved. We used to travel all over the country, playing charity matches and often going by coach on journeys which could be compared with a mobile Morecambe and Wise show, that is if our other player-cum-comedian was aboard. This was Ian Arthurs, who complemented John, making a double act that kept the rest of the team in stitches with laughter, so that by the time we eventually arrived at the match we had a ready-made excuse of exhaustion if we lost! In fact Ian was our star player who could be up to his ears in gin and tonic and still be relied upon to score a classic century without any apparent effort.

There was one occasion which John has failed to account, whether intentionally or not I don't know, but it happened after a match against the Oxford Downs when we were invited to supper with Ben and Pat Brooks. Buck decided that the time had come to liven up the proceedings, and he quietly disappeared upstairs to raid Mrs Brooks' wardrobe, reappearing in a most attractive short, frilly tennis dress. Now our hero has a shapely pair of legs, but he had forgotten that the only piece of underclothing he was wearing was a jockstrap!

It would be easy to ramble on about the good, the bad and the ugly bits of John Buckingham, but the idea is to read what he has written himself, so read on and enjoy it.

David Nicholson
Condicote, January 1987

INTRODUCTION

While I was helping John Buckingham to write this book I mentioned the fact to a friend of mine who used to ride occasionally as an amateur. He was delighted to hear that Buck was going into print and told me why.

'When I rode as an amateur Buck looked after me on three or four occasions,' my friend explained. 'He hardly knew who I was but he treated me in exactly the same way as he treated John Francome or any other top jockey. He gave the same amount of attention to every jockey he looked after and he made sure that we all left the weighing room looking immaculate. All in all he is very good at his job, and a super bloke.'

I think that just about sums up John Buckingham. Despite his great triumph at Aintree in 1967, he endured a lot of setbacks during his career, some of which would have floored a less resilient man. But he always bounced back and it is a measure of the respect in which his fellow jockeys held him that when the end of his riding days approached they rallied round to make sure that his future in racing was secured.

Writing this book with John has been a great pleasure. We have had a lot of laughs, and he has recounted a few stories which, sadly, we had best not reproduce here. He has struck me as a person who bears no malice, no ill-feeling towards his fellow man, but who is instead, as David Nicholson has said in his foreword, 'a genuine sort of guy.'

I have stood with him in the weighing room long after racing has finished and the jockeys and punters have headed home. I've watched him sweating over piles of muddy breeches and dirty boots, all the time chattering away about the day's results, cracking jokes, passing on any tips for future meetings. His pride in his job is as great as his enthusiasm for the sport, and I hope we have managed to convey some of that enthusiasm in this book.

John Dorman
January 1987

1

IN THE BEGINNING

In April 1955, when I was fifteen years old, my mother went to work for Mr & Mrs Edward Courage at their estate at Edgcote, near Banbury, on the borders of Oxfordshire and Northamptonshire. It was — and still is — a very large estate, consisting of a number of farms, some of which were tenanted, a big dairy and a sizeable stabling yard which in those days was famous for the quality of the steeplechasers bred there. Mr Courage was a member of the brewing family and was also involved in banking in the City. In his early thirties he had become paralysed from the waist down as the result of a polio attack, but that never prevented him from taking a very active interest in his horses, and he attended race meetings whenever his other business commitments allowed.

Soon after my mother went to Edgcote, I left school, with no idea what I was going to do in the future. It turned out that there were one or two opportunities for employment on the estate, and I was offered the choice of working with the sheep or the horses. I chose the horses — although I'll never know why. I knew nothing about sheep but at the same time I had never been near a horse in my life, let alone sat on one, and at first I was frightened to go into the stables. Still, whatever it was that made me choose working with the horses, it ultimately had a major effect on my whole life.

3

Jack and Tom Morgan were in charge of the stables. They had come to Edgcote in 1950 to look after Mr Courage's point-to-pointers and they had stayed on when he took out a trainer's permit a few years later. In fact they remained with the Courages all their working lives. They helped me to overcome my initial fear of horses, although they had to bodily push me into the stable block on one occasion, and having done this they taught me to ride, on a pony called Flicker. In those early days I was quite happy just being a simple stable lad, doing jobs like mucking out the boxes, sweeping the yard, feeding the horses. I had no thoughts at all of becoming a jockey.

For the first twelve months at Edgcote I lived with my mother — who had been divorced from my father a few years previously — my two brothers and my sister in a house on the estate. When my mother left I moved in with Tom Morgan, with whom I lodged for ten years. Jimmy Mumford was stable jockey then, and the yard's two class horses were Tiberetta and Tiberina, two brilliant mares who bred a string of class chasers, many of whom I was lucky enough to ride.

Late in 1955 I went to my first race meeting, at Chepstow, simply to help out with the horses and lead them around the paddock. That day was my first close association with the sport which has become my life. I was impressed with what I saw, I loved the atmosphere — I was hooked. I decided there and then that, if I was good enough, I was going to become a jockey.

In those days I knew nothing about race riding — I was more of a horseman than a jockey because that was the way I had been taught by Jack and Tom. I had been taught how to break in young horses, not how to ride a finish. I would have to learn that for myself. I used the saddlehorse in the yard, and later Mrs Courage gave me a copy of John Hislop's book *From Start to Finish*, which also taught me a lot about race riding.

I first sat on a racehorse in April 1956 when I started to ride work and school the horses over hurdles. Having

This must be one of the first pictures of me taken on a racecourse. The year is 1956, and as a sixteen-year-old stable boy I'm leading in Jimmy Mumford after he had won on Tetranard at Newton Abbot. Thirty years later only the jockeys' clothes would not look out of place.

made the decision to become a jockey I was naturally impatient to have my first ride under rules, and eventually Jack Morgan suggested to Mr Courage that I be given my chance. So, on 11 April 1957, I took part in my first race, riding Mr Courage's horse Royal Oak in a two-mile hurdle at Stratford-upon-Avon. We were unplaced but I was happy enough to have had the ride. I rode Royal Oak again three times that season, without success, and the following season I had four more rides on horses from the Courage stable, my best placing being third on Bob Scott at Towcester, which for us was the local course. Another young lad who worked for the Courages in those days was David Clayton. He was a nice chap and a promising young jockey who rode a winner for the stable at Towcester, but he later went out of the game when he began to have problems with his weight.

The next major milestone in the Buckingham career happened at Southwell on 26 March 1959. I rode my first winner, Sahagun, in a two-mile hurdle. It was only the sixteenth ride of my career. All in all the 1959/60 season was not too bad for this young jockey not yet out of his teens — I had three winners from thirty-one rides. I was lucky though, that I had no problems with my weight: I could always do 9 stone 7 easily so I got plenty of rides at the minimum weight. In fact it was only towards the end of my career in the saddle that I ever had to watch myself for a couple of days if I was due to do 10 stone. I have seen other jockeys go through agonies to do the minimum weight and I'm just glad that I never had serious problems in this area.

During those early years I was quite happy working at Edgcote and riding in the Courages' maroon and gold halved colours: in fact I didn't ride for anyone else until 1961. The Courage horses were always good jumpers, and I did most of their schooling; it was an excellent way to gain riding experience. After a few years I began to nurture the hope of becoming first jockey to the Courage stable, but that was never to be. David Nicholson had the job for a while, but basically I think that Mr Courage preferred to get a top jockey to ride his horses whenever he could, and in the early days people like Terry Biddle-combe and Matt McCourt also rode regularly for the stable. Nevertheless I did most of the early preparation, although in the middle sixties I was joined by 'Geordie' Mawson, a very good jockey who had come from Ryan Price's yard at Findon.

David Nicholson taught me a great deal about schooling horses. I've seen so many jockeys arrive at a yard in their

Despite the expression on my face, I was actually very fond of this horse. It is Sahagun, on whom I rode my first-ever winner, in March 1959. When I bought my house a few years later I named it after the horse.

car, jump on the horse, rush up to the gallops, whip the horse over the practice hurdles and then dash back to the car and get away again as quickly as possible. But David had all the time in the world. Instead of cantering he would say 'Steady, steady. *Walk* them up to the start of the gallops.' He believed that you had to make sure the horses were enjoying the job, or they wouldn't give of their best. He would walk them round nice and steady when they reached the gallops, before putting them over the practice hurdles.

In the Beginning

The Courages always had good horses, and bred some excellent jumpers. Over the years they won a number of major races, including the Hennessy, the Grand Annual Challenge Chase at the Cheltenham Festival meeting, the Topham at Aintree, the Champion Chase at Nottingham, the Black and White which used to be at Ascot, and many others. Mr Courage was the leading owner in the 1969/70 season, winning over £20,000 in prize money — a fair sum in those days. A lot of the best horses were bred by the two great mares Tiberetta and Tiberina, and among those I had the pleasure of riding were Lira, Neapolitan Lou, Royal Relief, San Angelo and Spanish Steps.

Spanish Steps is probably the most well known of all the Courage horses, and certainly the highest earner. He won a third of all the major races the stable picked up, including the Black and White in 1968 and the Hennessy in 1969. He was a small horse with a great big heart, and I was privileged to ride him for his first wins over both fences and hurdles. I later lost the ride, in an episode recounted elsewhere in this book, and it was one of the biggest disappointments of my career, although I did get to ride him again before he was retired. In his ten-year racing career between 1966 and 1976, Spanish Steps came under orders seventy-eight times, won on sixteen occasions, was placed on twenty-nine others, and won for his owners a total of £56,500 in prize money. He first ran at Chepstow in October 1966 when I partnered him in a two-mile hurdle, and his last race was the 1976 Grand National when he was ridden by my old mate Jeff King. In between

TOP
The position that every jockey likes to be in. The last has been safely jumped, we're about to pass the post, and the second horse is some lengths behind. This is me winning on Noble Pierre in December 1961 at Southwell, ironically one of my least favourite courses.

BOTTOM
The great mare Tiberetta, who bred — among others — Spanish Steps. We are posing outside the Courage home at Edgcote a few days after the 1958 Grand National.

times he was ridden by such leading jockeys as Jack Cook, Stan Mellor, Philip Blacker, Bill Smith and Richard Pitman, and I'm sure he gave a great deal of pleasure to thousands of racegoers.

TOP
Riding the great Spanish Steps to his first-ever victory — over the hurdles at Wolverhampton on a misty day in December 1966.

BOTTOM LEFT
John Francome wouldn't give this many marks for style. Spanish Steps again, winning over fences for the first time at Sandown in October 1968. I was proud of this particular 'double'. Following me are two jockeys who, I consider, were among the best at that time: David Mould (black cap) on Woodman, and Jeff King. Both were brilliantly strong finishers.

BELOW
A damp February day at Windsor in 1965, and I am leading over the water on the appropriately-named Damp Rag. Unfortunately this particular race ended in a pile of mud as far as I was concerned. Windsor was another course which I was never particularly fond of: it was always very wet due to its proximity to the River Thames, and the tight figure-of-eight circuit did not seem to suit a lot of horses.

Another very good horse bred by Tiberetta was Neapolitan Lou, seen here landing in front at Stratford in February 1965. We went on to win the two-mile chase.

Another favourite of mine in the early 1960s was Neapolitan Lou, out of Tiberina by Flush Royal. She was another small horse, only 15.1 hands, but again she was tough. I rode her to nine of her ten victories, and on 14 May 1962 she completed my first ever double. In March 1965 she won the Watney Mann's Red Barrel Chase at Market Rasen without being headed, and, of course, it was particularly pleasing that the prize money came from a rival brewer! A fortnight later another brewer was having to part with money to the Courages, when Neapolitan Lou won the Fremlins Handicap Chase at Folkestone. This win was even better as far as I was concerned, because the jockey's prize was thirty-six pints of beer!

Of all the Courage horses, and indeed all the horses I ever rode, I think that San Angelo was my favourite. It is a painting of me riding him, rather than Foinavon, which

Mr Courage was especially pleased in March 1965 when Neapolitan Lou and I won the Watney Mann Red Barrel Chase at Market Rasen, since it enabled him to take some decent prize money plus a silver salver off a rival brewer. (ABOVE) Harry Anson is leading us into the winner's enclosure and (BELOW) Mr and Mrs Courage at the presentation.

A month after our victory in the Watney Mann Red Barrel Chase the same combination was at it again, this time at Folkestone where we won the Fremlins Brewery Handicap. John Rickman of ITA Television is interviewing me afterwards, with Mrs Courage acting as interpreter. It was one of my first ever interviews, but my rather glazed look has nothing to do with nerves: it was more likely in anticipation of the winning jockey's prize — thirty-six pints of Fremlins best bitter! Fortunately I wasn't having to waste at the time.

hangs over my living-room fireplace. In his early days he won a couple of novice chases under Terry Biddlecombe, but I rode him to all his other victories, including the 1967 Grand Annual Challenge Chase at the Cheltenham Festival meeting. I believe that certain horses work well for certain jockeys, and this was certainly true of San Angelo and me.

14

Judging by the expression on my face, I have put in a lot of hard work for nothing. Attribute at Towcester in 1967.

In 1964 the most important event of my life occurred. I went to a dance at Chesford Grange in Leamington Spa, and there I met Ann. We saw each other regularly after that and were married in September 1966. I had been

A recent picture of Ann, Laura, Lucy and myself, with a few mementos from my riding days.

saving money through a scheme run by the Jockeys' Association, and we bought a brand new house on a modern estate in Chipping Warden, a village just a few miles from Edgcote. It cost less than £3,500 which these days wouldn't pay for the cost of adding an extra room! We called the house Sahagun, after my first winner, and we're still living there twenty-one years later with our daughters Laura and Lucy. I don't suppose we will ever move now.

At the time of writing, Spanish Steps is still alive and living in contented retirement on the Courage estate. Ann and I occasionally take our dog for a walk down there, and it is always a pleasure to see him looking so well. It brings back some happy memories too. Tiberetta and Tiberina

16

are buried side by side in a field on the estate, and one day Spanish Steps will join them. That will be the end of an era. When Jack Morgan died in 1986, his ashes were scattered over the graves of the two great mares, and I know that he would have been immensely pleased about that.

Mr Courage died in the summer of 1982. His death was a great loss to jump racing, for despite his disability he had played a very active role in the sport, and, of course, he had bred such a string of good horses. Mrs Courage still lives at Edgcote, although there are no longer any horses in training there.

All in all I had a very happy association with the Courage family, and I still rode their horses occasionally after I turned freelance in 1969. The last Courage horse I rode was Pride of Kentucky, in a four-mile chase at Uttoxeter in May 1970, and a month earlier I had ridden him in the Grand National. It is that famous race and my earlier success there which is the subject of the next chapter of this book.

2

FOINAVON, APRIL 1967

Foinavon has no chance. Not the boldest of jumpers, he can safely be ignored, even in a race noted for shocks. Charles Benson, *Daily Express*, Saturday, 8 April 1967

It all began three days before the race, on the morning of Wednesday, 5 April. Many jockeys were starting to feel a little excited and possibly a little nervous too with the Grand National approaching, but I wasn't due to go to Liverpool at all. I had no booked rides for the entire three days of the meeting and instead I was due to ride a couple for Jack Peacock at Worcester on the Saturday.

At ten o'clock that Wednesday morning I was getting ready to go to my uncle's funeral. Funnily enough I had heard a story not long before about a trainer who was driving to Liverpool and passed a funeral procession. Later that day his horse won, so the next time that he went to Liverpool he drove around until he found another funeral procession, and the horse won again. Anyway, however significant that may be, I was knotting my black tie when the telephone rang. It was John Kempton, Foinavon's trainer, and he came straight to the point and asked me if I would ride Foinavon in the National on Saturday.

Of course, I jumped at the chance. I had never ridden in the National before, and I had more or less resigned myself to the fact that I never would. I had been to Aintree on quite a few occasions to help look after the Courage horses, and I had thought rather wistfully how nice it would be to ride in the world's greatest steeplechase, but at the same time I believed it was just a pipe-dream. I had actually ridden the National course, because during the same meeting the previous year I had picked up a spare ride in the Topham on a horse called Happy Henry. I had also ridden Foinavon before, in a four-mile chase at Cheltenham in March 1966, and although we were unplaced the horse had given me a good ride over Cheltenham's difficult fences.

John Kempton asked me to come to Taunton to ride a couple for him the following day, when we would also be able to talk about Foinavon. One of the first things he told me was that two other jockeys — Ron Atkins and Bruce Gregory — had both turned down the ride because they considered that they weren't being offered enough money for it. Quite often jockeys are offered a few quid extra to ride in the National but John Kempton explained that the owners, Mr and Mrs Watkins, did not want to pay an extra £200 or so just to see the horse pulled up after only a few fences. Later, Mr Watkins himself told me that he would pay according to how the horse ran, which I reckoned was fair enough. To be honest, I would have done it for nothing if necessary, just to have a ride in the National. Having sorted that out, I then had to ring Jack Peacock and ask him if he would mind if I didn't fulfil my commitments to him at Worcester that coming Saturday. He was delighted to let me off.

The next problem was finding somewhere to stay in Liverpool; all the regular digs were full at this stage. Eventually I found some people I knew who lived near the course. They had some room but warned me that it wouldn't be very comfortable, so Ann decided to stay behind and watch the race on television with her grandmother who lived in Leamington Spa. My brother Tom came up to Liverpool with me to provide the moral support. It was just as well that Ann didn't come — I spent the night before the Grand National sleeping on two armchairs pushed together! Somehow it is difficult to imagine Hywel Davies or Richard Dunwoody doing that nowadays.

Very few of Foinavon's connections bothered to make the trip either. Mr and Mrs Watkins watched the race on television rather than travelling all the way from Surrey, and John Kempton went to Worcester, where he was due to ride, and left his father in charge of things at Aintree. I suppose that with the horse quoted at 100-1 they weren't expecting any fireworks. There were no pre-planned tactics — Jack Kempton simply said to keep him handy with the rest of the field as long as I could.

I was quite nervous in the weighing room as I pulled on the owners' very distinctive colours of black, with red and yellow braces and hooped cap. After we had weighed out, the preliminaries in the parade ring and then on the course itself seemed to take ages, but at last we came under orders. I had positioned myself between the inner and the middle.

The tapes went up and we were one of the first away: in fact we jumped the first fence more or less in front. After that the field began to string out a bit as the front-running horses went off at a helluva good gallop, and I never stopped pushing and kicking from then on. I don't remember a great deal about the first circuit because I was concentrating hard on keeping Foinavon going and staying out of trouble at the same time. I tucked in behind Josh Gifford who was on the 15-2 favourite, Honey End. In my opinion Josh was one of the best judges of pace in his time so I was quite happy to sit behind him, and in fact he was only three lengths in front of me at Becher's Brook second time round. We were a long way back from the leaders but

The famous Foinavon colours — black, red and yellow braces, red and yellow hooped cap.

This is the second or third fence on the first circuit, Foinavon (number 38) is on the extreme right. We had led over the first but now some of the early pacemakers are beginning to kick on. They went at such a gallop that I thought they were bound to come back to us eventually, and I'm sure that at least two of them could have jumped through the mêlée at the 23rd, but they stopped out of pure exhaustion.

I thought 'They'll come back to us, they'll never keep that pace up,' and I was confident about Josh's judgement of the pace. As I cleared Becher's on the second circuit I saw him landing, so I was happy that we were still going pretty well. The only difference was that Honey End would probably have a bit in reserve at the end of the race, whereas Foinavon might prove to be one-paced.

Then everything changed very suddenly.

As I came up to the 23rd fence, the smallest on the course, I was suddenly aware that I was galloping into a solid wall of horses. They were everywhere — straddling the fence, turning round, running back towards me. There were loose horses trotting up and down alongside the fence and the jockeys running up and down trying to retrieve them. The whole area was a complete shambles.

FOINAVON, APRIL 1967

I was just far enough behind not to get caught up in the thick of it. I had to make an instant decision, so I steered Foinavon to the right — the outside — to get away from the main part of the mêlée. There was a small gap in the fence that was unaffected by the pile-up and we approached it at a forty-five degree angle. At that stage I had no idea whether anyone else had jumped the fence or not and I was purely concerned about carrying on if I possibly could. Foinavon had reduced to a canter and he jumped the fence off his hocks like a showjumper. I kicked on away from the fence and realized then that we were in front.

After that I knew that if we could keep going we would win it, but it was not a case of thinking 'I'm going to win the National!' and relaxing. Foinavon was unfamiliar with the fences and tried to duck out once or twice, so I never stopped working on him. Josh Gifford had been hampered by the confusion but towards the end of the race he got a fair way back to me. Thankfully, Foinavon jumped the last well and produced a good gallop as we came past the elbow and up to the line.

As we passed the post I felt very relieved, and extremely tired, because it had been such hard work. People ran on to the track, and two mounted policemen took up station on either side of me to escort me to the winners' enclosure. It suddenly dawned on me that I had won the Grand National!

The pile-up had been caused by a loose horse, Popham Down, which had fallen at the first fence. He had run right across the 23rd. The two horses who had made most of the running at such a fast gallop could, I reckon, have jumped the fence, but instead they just stopped, maybe grateful for any excuse to do so. The horses on their outside cannoned into Popham Down, and that produced a catastrophic chain reaction. At that stage of the race the television cameras were recording a side-on view from just behind the fence and the effect of the horses coming into the fence is just like a concertina with the fence itself

Continued on page 26

23

The moment I became a national celebrity (no pun intended). I am (arrowed) in the top right of the picture, in the dark colours with the light braces. Foinavon has just popped over the 23rd fence and we are on our way to make history, while behind us all is chaos. Immediately behind me Josh Gifford (dark colours with light sleeves) is having to whip the favourite, Honey End, round to have a second crack at the fence — a manoeuvre which cost him the race — while behind him Paul Kelleway (spotted cap) is doing the same on What a Myth.

The jockey in the quartered colours on the extreme left of the picture is Johnny Haine, who actually jumped the fence cleanly on Rondetto some time before I did, but tripped up on landing. It was my lucky day, not his. I'm not sure why Johnny is waving his arms in the air, unless he's asking if he can have a second go at it. In the dark

colours with the light crossbelts is Ken White, and immediately behind him you can see Paddy Broderick about to remount Kertel Lad. They finished. Horse number 9, on its side next to Ken, actually got stuck in the fence and had to be physically hauled out.

In the centre of the picture, facing the camera and looking rather mournful, is Brian Fletcher on Red Alligator. They eventually jumped the fence too and finished third behind Josh and me. The following year the same combination did even better — they won the race, and Brian won it twice more after that on Red Rum.

As you can see, the fence itself has been comprehensively demolished, and the crowd on the rails seems suitably awestruck. If the mounted policeman (top centre) had jumped out on to the course he would have had a head start on all of us!

as the box. One horse — Rondetto ridden by Johnny Haine — actually jumped the fence in the middle of all this but tripped up as he landed on the other side.

The angle of the cameras then switched to a position in front of the fence and for a long time all you can see is a seething mass of horses and jockeys going in all directions, until Foinavon pops up on the outside, jumps the fence and hacks away from it. For quite a few seconds the 1967 Grand National almost came to a halt.

I had been about thirty lengths behind the leaders when the mêlée occurred, although because of the very fast pace this had not worried me too much. Josh was less fortunate. Slightly in front of me at the 23rd, he had no time at all to decide what to do. He went for the middle, found he had to stop, so whipped round and had a second go. It cost him valuable time, but having watched the video of the race hundreds of times since, I realise that he made up an incredible amount of ground on Honey End and was really quite close to me as we jumped the last. Nevertheless I think that great credit must be given to Foinavon for jumping the 23rd at all after what he saw there. A lot of horses would have pulled up.

There is a photograph of me being led into the winners' enclosure with an expression on my face which is a mixture of elation and exhaustion. That is precisely how I felt. The magnitude of the event was beginning to sink in but it was going to take a long time to do so fully. I weighed in and the valet took my saddle away — as I have done to many other winning jockeys since — then I was ushered into the press room. People were firing questions at me from all directions and I answered them as best I could but the whole thing was a bit bewildering. Nothing

Jumping the last in the 1967 National. I know now that only a fall can prevent us from winning, and I'm sitting well back. The final fence at Aintree is not as easy as it might look, with a nasty little dip on landing. To lose the race there would have been a tragedy.

I've won the National! Here I am being led in off the course, exhausted but exultant.

like this had ever happened to me before and I never thought that it would, so I was simply not prepared for it.

I finally got out of the press room and went back to the weighing room where there was a good deal of back-slapping and congratulations from the other jockeys — such is the camaraderie of jump racing. There was an envelope addressed to The Winner, The Grand National. I opened it and inside was an invitation to appear the following evening on *Sunday Night at the Palladium*, which was the top television variety show at the time, compèred by Bob Monkhouse. I called for champagne and Josh opened the first bottle. He split the cork and put half a crown in it, then handed it to me and said 'Well done, John.' He must have been bitterly disappointed, and I thought it was a marvellous gesture.

Later on, when he was interviewed about the race, Josh said he could only have won if I'd fallen. Some pressmen misinterpreted this and accused Josh of being bitter about it all. They said that his attitude smacked of sour grapes, but I think they were wrong. You are naturally going to be disappointed if a 100-1 outsider beats you on the favourite but I don't believe that Josh meant any ill. He was dead right — he would only have won if I'd fallen!

★   ★   ★

In those days anyone who had something to celebrate after the National would go to the Adelphi in Liverpool, but I wasn't prepared for that. In any case, the people connected with the horse weren't there. Fortunately, John Kempton had managed to see the race on television at Worcester and he had also ridden a winner there, so all in all he had a pretty good day.

Outside the weighing room I found my brother Tom, who was smelling of whisky — most unusual for a virtual teetotaller! Then I telephoned Jack Morgan at Edgcote. I said 'What do you think of that then?', and he said something like 'Bloody marvellous.' I asked him to get everyone round to the pub because Tom and I were about to leave the course. When I got home the neighbours had been busy. They had decorated the front of our house with flags and 'Well done, John' signs, and had painted the words 'Buckingham Palace' on the windows. I then went to our local pub which was packed out with people. Ann was there, and my friends from the village and all the lads from Edgcote. We had a great party that night, and it was good to celebrate such a triumphant moment with them all.

Of course that was not the end of the matter, and I found that I had suddenly become a national celebrity — as had Foinavon. The following day I went up to London to do the Palladium show. I met Bob Monkhouse, who was a charming man, and we rehearsed my part of the evening. When the time came to go on live though, I was more nervous than I had been at any other time of my life, and they virtually had to push me on to the stage! The media were constantly after me, and Foinavon and I appeared at various fêtes and shows. I also rode him past the real Buckingham Palace and up The Mall to be presented to the Duchess of Kent. I was guest of honour at a special dinner at the World Sporting Club in London, where Lord Derby presented me with a trophy to commemorate my win. That particular evening was a stag do, and Josh, Terry Biddlecombe and David Mould were sitting opposite me at the top table. I heard one of them say 'Get Buck on the brandy,' and then when the dinner was over they took me out on the town. I was just a simple country boy but those chaps knew all the places to visit and although my memory of it is a little hazy, we must have had one helluva night because I missed riding first lot the next morning!

A few days later Mr and Mrs Watkins gave a special party at their home in Surrey which was attended by John

Every National-winning horse and jockey combination has to per-
form a few publicity stunts and ours, as you can see, was not a
particularly low-key one. Foinavon was tacked up in Buckingham
Palace Mews and then, with her permanent companion Susie the goat,
we were led past Buckingham Palace itself and up The Mall.

Kempton and his wife, Ann and myself and the ex-joint
owners of Foinavon.

Apart from all the celebrating and public appearances
normal life had to continue, and on the Monday after the
Grand National I went to Wye where I was unplaced on
my only ride. On the Tuesday I had two thirds and a
second at Plumpton, but it was a whole six weeks before I
rode another winner. I always used to go to courses like
Plumpton by train because it took too long by car going
across country in the days before motorways. On this
occasion I went with David Sunderland who lived quite
close to me. As we were on our way to the Underground
at Paddington, I heard a little boy behind me saying 'Go

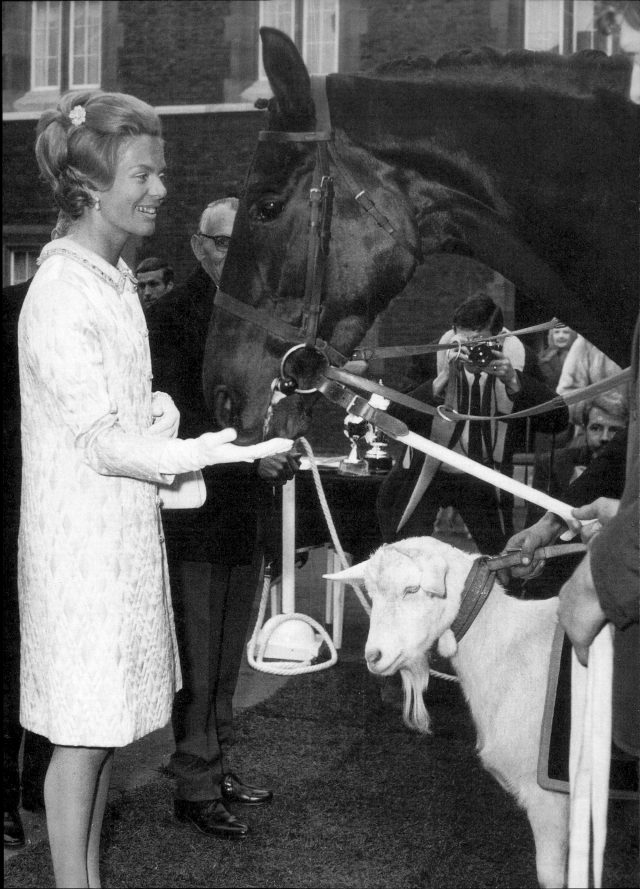

ABOVE
After I won the National I was in great demand for opening fêtes and shows. This is the opening of Pulford school fête in 1967. Ann is on my right, and the man on the pony is Bob Trudgill, who won the 1924 Grand National on Master Robert.

LEFT
After our parade up The Mall, Foinavon and Susie met the Duchess of Kent outside St James's Palace.

on, mum, ask him!', and I was asked for my autograph. I had never been recognised in public like that before. When we got to Victoria station we had plenty of time before the Plumpton train so we went for a haircut and one of those smashing hot shaves that you can only get in an old-fashioned barber's shop. David had his first and paid his five bob, or whatever it was. But when I was finished, the barber said 'That's all right, Mr Buckingham, there'll be no charge.' David was not very amused! When we reached Plumpton Ron Atkins and Bruce Gregory were there, and both immediately congratulated me.

Stoneleigh Show 1967. I seem to be keeping most of the crowd amused.

What would have happened if there had not been that huge pile-up at the 23rd fence? We will never know, of course, but I am convinced that Foinavon would not in different circumstances have disgraced himself. We were still going pretty well at the 23rd, and I am sure that the front runners, who were going at such a gallop, would have come back to us before the finish. We weren't going well enough to win, or even to be in the first four, but we would have been in the first ten or twelve. I don't believe that Josh, with his fine judgement of pace, would have let Honey End get so far behind the leaders if he hadn't thought he could catch them, and I wasn't too far behind Josh at that stage. Still, one can speculate forever about what might have happened. As far as I'm concerned the result is in the record book, and that's what counts!

Foinavon was my eleventh winner of the season, and the forty-fifth of my career. The 23rd fence at Aintree has now been officially named after the horse.

3

AFTER FOINAVON

After I had won the 1967 Grand National I got quite a few offers of extra rides, as is usually the case with a National-winning jockey, and, indeed, that season turned out to be my busiest ever, with a total of one hundred and eighty rides. The following season, 1967/8, should have been very busy too, but I broke my arm in a fall at Worcester in March — ironically when riding a John Kempton-trained horse — and missed the next two months. It also meant missing the National, of course, which was a great disappointment. John Kempton had already asked me to ride Foinavon again, but Mr Courage had claimed me for San Angelo, so either way I had been looking forward to a good race. Anyway, I took Ann up to Liverpool with me and we watched the race from the Chair fence. Foinavon was going quite well, ridden by Phil Harvey, and was still in touch when he was brought down at the water.

By August 1968 I was fully fit again and looking forward to the new season. Foinavon and I were reunited on 22 August at Devon and Exeter, where we were fourth in a three-mile chase, and two weeks later we came third on the same course. At our third attempt there, on 18 September, my Grand National-winning partner gave me my first win of the season. All in all I rode twenty winners in the 1968/9 season, from one hundred and sixty-nine rides. For the National that season I was without a ride until a week before the race, when Bob Turnell rang me.

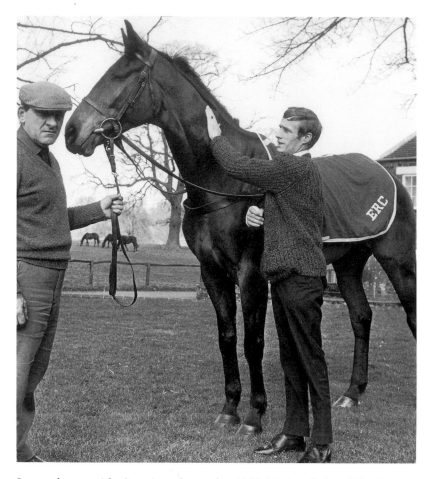

I was due to ride San Angelo in the 1968 National, but I broke my forearm a month beforehand. In this picture I'm not sure if I'm telling the horse how lucky he is not to have me guiding him round Aintree, or commiserating with him for not having last year's winning jockey on his back. Judging by Tom Morgan's expression, it's probably the latter.

He trained a horse called Limeburner, and he had been hoping that his son Andy would ride it, but Andy had been claimed by Derek Ancil to ride Kellesboro Wood. Of course I was happy to accept Bob's offer, and Limeburner gave me a super ride. The horse had not been to Liverpool before, but his jumping improved a great deal after the first circuit, and we finished eleventh, which convinced me that Limeburner had a great future as a National horse. Eddie Harty won the race on Highland Wedding.

National Hunt racing can be a cruel sport, with the elation of a victory followed swiftly by the disappointment of a defeat, or the pain of a broken limb. Two things happened during that 1968/9 which, although they did not involve any physical pain, were particularly hard to bear and ultimately had a big influence on my decision to leave the Courage stable and turn freelance.

The first was being jocked off Spanish Steps. I can understand how Phil Tuck must have felt when he was jocked off Burrough Hill Lad, and what Tony Mullins must have gone through — he has probably lost count of the number of times he was jocked off Dawn Run.

The 1969 Grand National, Becher's Brook, second time round. I am on Limeburner (number 28). He had never been to Liverpool before and after the first circuit he jumped really well. We finished eleventh, and I marked him down as a good horse for Liverpool in the future. I was lying second on him in 1971 when we fell at the second-last. The jockey on the far left is adopting a rather forward-looking 'crouch'!

However philosophical you are, however hard you try to hide your feelings from yourself as well as the public, it is always a deep disappointment to lose a ride on a really class horse. Even the great John Francome has been jocked off horses, but being Francome he was jocked off quite a few at the same time and not because of any doubts about his riding ability. He lost the rides on all the horses that Sheikh Ali Abu Khamsin had in training with Fred Winter, and I understand that the decision was not entirely unconnected with the fact that John awarded the owner the nickname of 'Sooty'.

Spanish Steps, who came from that great mare Tiberetta, was without question one of the best horses the Courages ever bred. I schooled Spanish Steps, and I rode him when he first won over hurdles, at Wolverhampton, and again when he won his first chase, at Sandown. In October 1968 I rode Spanish Steps on his first outing of the season at Sandown, and we won easily. Then, three weeks later at the same course, we were beaten into second place when we should have won. Looking back on it, Spanish Steps was such a good horse that maybe I got a bit cocky on him. Anyway, I didn't ride him again for some months because shortly afterwards Jack Cook was sitting next to Mrs Courage at a dinner and like any sensible jockey he took the opportunity to pitch for the ride — and he got it.

The second big disappointment during that season was not having a single ride on my favourite horse, San Angelo. I was never given any reason for not getting the mount on him, and to this day I have been unable to think of one. As I said in an earlier chapter, I believe that certain

A rare occasion when San Angelo and I were not working well together. This is the 'Hurry On' Handicap Steeplechase at Ascot in November 1967, and I am certainly 'hurrying on' out of the side door, the most annoying thing about it is that I was five lengths clear at the time. The dreaded initials U R went down beside my name that day. Throughout my riding career I never won at Ascot.

San Angelo in action at Towcester in 1967. We eventually finished second in this two-and-a-half-mile chase.

horses run well for certain jockeys, and that San Angelo and I had that special understanding. As it turned out he never looked like winning during that 1968/9 season, and the nearest he got to it was when finishing third under 'Geordie' Mawson in an apprentice race at Chepstow.

One incident that cheered me up during that rather depressing final season with the Courage stable involved a horse called Boatman, trained by Stan Roberts, for whom I had a lot of outside rides. It was February 1969 and Boatman was entered for Windsor on the 26th and for Wincanton the following day. Stan decided the best policy was to run him at Windsor, because the race at Wincanton was the Kingswell Hurdle — regarded as a Champion Hurdle trial — and the great Persian War was down to run in it.

Just before I mounted Boatman in the parade ring Stan gave me instructions not to knock him about in order to win, so I gave him an easy ride, but we won anyway. I had two more rides for Stan that day but nothing booked for the following day, so I was looking forward to an afternoon with my feet up.

The following morning the phone rang at six o'clock. It was Stan.

'We're going to Wincanton with Boatman today,' he said.

'What!'

'Yes. He's still fresh, he's eaten up well, so get in your car.'

I thought he was mad, but he was the guv'nor, so I got

Boatman clears the last at Wincanton on 27 February 1969, just ahead of Persian War (Jimmy Uttley). He went on to beat this much-fancied horse, having also won at Windsor the previous day. I wonder how many other times a horse has won two races in twenty-four hours.

Sooner or later every jockey bears the consequences of going novice chasing. Here it is my turn in the Burford Novices Chase at Newbury in March 1969, as I part company with Chinaman at the open ditch. It was a spare ride, and one that I would have done better to turn down.

in my car and headed for the West Country. Like everyone else in the race I didn't fancy my chances against Persian War, but I was upsides him coming to the last, and we went away to win the race. Stan's confidence had been fully vindicated, and he and I were dead chuffed about it!

It is a very rare feat indeed for a horse to win two races on two consecutive days, and I was looking forward to some good press coverage the next morning. Unfortunately, most of the journalists virtually ignored Boatman's great achievement, and instead wrote paragraphs about Persian War's defeat. It was even suggested that Persian War had had a temperature, but if that was the case his trainer would not have run him. As far as I am concerned, Boatman beat him fair and square.

Throughout the 1968/9 season I had only six rides for the Courage stable, which is not very good for a retained jockey. One of those six was especially pleasant though, for in April 1969 Jack Cook was unable to ride Spanish Steps in the Whitbread Gold Cup at Sandown, and I was teamed up with my old pal again, to finish third. However, I had already decided that from the start of the 1969/70 season I would turn freelance.

I am not sure if that was the right thing to do. My problem throughout my career was that I never pushed hard enough for rides, something which is vital for a freelance jockey. If someone offered me a ride I nearly always accepted, but I should have spent more time on the telephone hustling for spare rides. If your name is Winter, or Francome, or Scudamore you get offered more rides than you can possibly accept, but the average jump jockey cannot afford to wait for the telephone to ring. I suppose that pushing myself forward was something which was against my nature, but in retrospect I think I should have overcome that and got after the owners and trainers.

★　★　★

So my freelance career began in August 1969 and produced a winner from my second ride, a horse called Silver Lily in a two-and-a-half-mile chase at Newton Abbot. The same horse won for me again over the distance at the same course a fortnight later. I knew that I could expect a fair few rides from trainers I had been associated with in the past, like Ken Bailey, John Kempton, Jack Peacock, Stan Roberts and Stan Wright, and although I was no longer retained by Mr Courage I was still riding out for the yard, so I hoped for one or two rides from him as well.

I was delighted when he asked me to ride San Angelo in a two-mile chase at Sandown in November. I had not ridden the horse for eighteen months but we instantly clicked again and won the two-horse race by a good many lengths from the favourite, JFK. In fact, we won so well that I think there was almost a fence separating us at the end. I was immediately asked to ride San Angelo again at Cheltenham the following weekend. I looked forward to it with pleasure — the horse was well handicapped and I was confident we would win again.

The night before the Cheltenham meeting the annual jockeys' dinner took place at the Queen's Hotel in the town. I was talking to Stan Mellor when he said that he had to go and telephone Mr Courage. I asked him why, and he told me it was because Mr Courage wanted him to ride San Angelo the following day. This was news to me and I was shocked. I had done nothing wrong on the horse at Sandown the previous weekend, and nobody had said a word to me about not riding him at Cheltenham. In fact, I had turned down two rides at Windsor and one for Stan Wright at Cheltenham in the same race, because San Angelo was the pick of the four I had been offered.

TOP
Silver Lily (number 5) provided me with my first winner in only my second ride after I had turned freelance at the beginning of the 1969/70 season. Here we clear the water second time round at Newton Abbot. If I had kept up that sort of momentum as a freelance I might have carried on riding longer than I did.

BOTTOM
On the gallops at Edgcote with San Angelo, my favourite horse. This is where so much of the hard preparation work is done.

Stan Mellor was a bit embarrassed about the whole situation and he suggested that I went to the phone box with him to see if we could sort the thing out. When we got through to Mr Courage he confirmed that he wanted Stan to ride San Angelo because of his greater experience. Well, it was true that he had been riding longer than me, and had been Champion Jockey three times, but after twelve years in the saddle myself, I reckoned I knew my way around a racecourse. It seemed a rather lame excuse. Anyway, there was nothing for it but to contact my other trainers to explain what had happened, or they would have wanted to know why I had turned down rides for them when I had nothing else booked.

The following day, despite having no rides, I went to Cheltenham. I watched Stan Mellor jump four fences on San Angelo and then pull up. I turned away, bitterly disappointed. I was never to ride San Angelo again.

The season produced ten winners out of one hundred and thirty-four rides, which was not as good as I had either expected or hoped. Despite being a freelance I was not getting offered many rides from trainers with whom I was not already associated, and that was a bit worrying. However, I went to Aintree to ride Pride of Kentucky for the Courages in the National, hoping for soft ground. Pride of Kentucky loved the heavy going but unfortunately that year the going was good, otherwise I think we might have finished there or thereabouts. As it was we finished sixth, and Pat Taafe won the race on Gay Trip. A month later I rode Pride of Kentucky again in a four-mile

TOP
I rode a lot of horses for John Kempton, and Glory Stream, seen here at Cheltenham in September 1969, provided me with three winners in the early part of that season. Terry Biddlecombe and Tommy Stack are following.

BOTTOM
Glory Stream in the old parade ring at Cheltenham after winning there in November 1969. John and Bridget Kempton are on the left of the picture.

chase at Uttoxeter. We were unplaced, and it turned out to be my last ever ride for Mr Courage.

At the start of the 1970/1 season the future looked bleak. I knew then that I was not going to get the number of rides I was hoping for, and the chances were that at the end of the season I would have to pack it up. At the same time I had no idea what I was going to do for a living. The only thing I did know was that I wanted to stay in racing if I could, because it had been my life.

It was a desperate season. I had only eighty-seven rides, and sixty-seven of those either fell or were unplaced. I had just one winner, at Warwick on a horse called Tea For Two. It was an easy win really, when you consider that no other horse finished the race! What happened was that a horse fell on the back straight and had to be destroyed. When we came round the second time the wretched animal was still on the ground so there was a flag up to warn us of the danger. But someone else was waving a second flag which confused all the other horses and they refused, while I jumped the fence and finished.

With not many rides and even fewer winners the bank balance was hardly very healthy that season. I had a small retainer from John Webber, who also trains near Banbury, and if it had not been for that I don't know how I would have kept going. I shall always be grateful to John for having faith in me.

I went to Aintree on 3 April for what I knew was my last National. I was back on Limeburner, and I knew we were in with a chance. We were in front at the Canal Turn second time round before Jack Cook went ahead on Specify, the eventual winner. Coming to the second last I was upsides Black Secret, but Limeburner fell. It was very frustrating, because although I remounted and finished, I am sure we would have been in the frame but for that fall.

Nevertheless I am proud of my Grand National record, which although short is still pretty good. Some jockeys never have a decent ride at Liverpool — David Nicholson and Jonjo O'Neill are just two examples of this. Some

Pride of Kentucky in Mr Courage's yard, with me in my working gear of flat cap, sweater and wellies. I rode the old horse many times. He loved the soft ground, and if the going had been softer at Aintree I think we would have done better than finishing sixth in the 1970 National.

horses don't take to Aintree at all, but I was lucky enough to ride some good Liverpool horses.

Unbeknown to me at this time, things were being done on my behalf which were going to solve the problems of the future. The fellowship and camaraderie of the weighing room was working. Some of my fellow jockeys, among them David Nicholson and Richard Pitman, had

John Webber at his house near Banbury. If he hadn't given me a small retainer during my final season as a jockey I would have been really struggling.

approached the Jockeys' Association and told them that I might have to pack up, at the same time suggesting that the jockeys could do with an extra valet. The Jockeys' Association then rang me up about it, and, of course, I accepted. Under Jockey Club rules, I should have served a three-year apprenticeship under a Master Valet before applying for a Master Valet's licence myself, but the Jockey Club waived that regulation and I was in.

My last race was at Wetherby during an evening

meeting in May 1971. The horse's owner was a friend of mine, Denis Everett, and we agreed to meet beforehand at Bawtry roundabout near Doncaster. I left my car by a cafe there and Denis drove me up to Wetherby, together with George Lee, another jockey who at the time was on crutches as the result of a broken left leg.

During the race I fell at the second last and injured my right knee. Once I had got changed, it felt worse and was beginning to stiffen up. Denis drove us back to the cafe where I had left my car, by which time my knee was very bad indeed. When Denis stopped the car, George got out on his crutches and went over to my car, getting into the front passenger seat. Denis then brought the crutches back to me, and I hobbled over and got into the driver's seat. The customers in the cafe couldn't believe what they were seeing! George and I, between us, then drove the car down to his place in Stamford — I worked the accelerator and brake with my left foot and George worked the clutch with his right foot. All in all it was quite an interesting journey. The following morning I had to be driven home to Banbury, where they put my leg into plaster. Thus ended the riding career of J. Buckingham!

★   ★   ★

I started valeting at the beginning of the 1971/2 jumping season. I had gone into partnership with another ex-jockey, Steve Rooney, and we decided to give the venture three years. After that time, if we didn't like the job or we weren't making any headway, we would pack it up and do something else. In fact, Steve did stop after three years, because he felt the work didn't suit him, but I continued and took on my brother Tom as a partner. We've been together ever since.

To begin with I was virtually flat broke, because I had to invest a lot of money in buying tack, which every valet has to carry, and a reliable car. We also had to get jockeys, of course, and this meant some of them had to leave their

I started valeting at the beginning of the 1971/2 season, and here I am in the weighing room at Ludlow with Graham Thorner, who was then Champion Jockey.

current valets, which caused a rather tense atmosphere in the weighing room for the first few months. In addition, we were travelling long distances, and therefore spending a fair bit on petrol, initially to do just two or three jockeys. I remember one night, when in between meetings at Fontwell and Plumpton, we stopped with some relatives of Steve's near Brighton. Before we went to bed we turned out our pockets and found that we had two shillings and sixpence between us. In today's money that's twelve and a half pence! That wasn't going to get us very far, so the following day I had to ask Henry Kavanagh, a super bloke, if he wouldn't mind paying for his ride there and then. Of course he obliged and we were able to buy enough petrol to get home.

During this period I received a telephone call from Brough Scott, another jockey who had packed in riding not long after I did. He called to say that he was passing through Banbury later in the week and could we meet. When we did he took me to his car and opened the boot. In there were two saddles, two pairs of boots, two pairs of breeches, his crash helmet and various other bits and pieces.

'That's all my racing stuff,' he said. 'I don't need it anymore. You have it.'

'That's very kind of you,' I said. 'How much do you want for it?'

'Nothing,' replied Brough. 'It's yours. Take it.'

He knew about my dicey finances at the time, and I thought it was a superb gesture.

Certainly those days were a struggle, and Ann had to be very careful with the housekeeping money, but we gradually began to get more jockeys and things started to look up. David Nicholson began training and sent all his jockeys to me, as did Josh Gifford. Nowadays I've got so many jockeys to look after that I'm rushed off my feet at big meetings, but it does give me a great deal of pride to 'do' the winner of a big race like the Gold Cup or the National, and I have been responsible for the last three winners of the Aintree race.

Of course, as a valet, I do a tremendously high mileage: I reckon on average around 50,000 miles a year, although some of this is done in my brother's car. Nevertheless I have to change my own car pretty frequently if I'm to get a decent trade-in price, and I usually have a new car every eighteen months. All in all I must have owned nearly a dozen cars since I started valeting. I've had Corsairs, Capris, Chrysler 180s, Cavaliers and my last five cars have been the BMW 5 series. I would actually prefer not to have to spend so much money on a car, but I must have something that is both roomy and reliable. People ask me why I don't buy a big station wagon and my reply is that I have enough tack to carry around as it is: if I bought a station wagon the jockeys would be asking me to carry all sorts of extra bits and pieces and I would have to spend an extra hour every day unloading and loading it. As it is now, I have to take the back seat out of the BMW Certainly, the BMWs have been thoroughly reliable. In all the years that I've owned them I have only had trouble once. It was a minor thing but, according to the Law of Sod, it happened when I was on my way to one of the most important engagements of my career. All is revealed in Chapter 9 of this book.

Over the years I've had the odd bump, been caught speeding, and was once breathalysed. I had one car which I'm sure was jinxed from the moment it left the showroom. It was a blue Corsair and the only part of it that didn't need panel-beating and respraying in the time I owned it was the roof. It got scraped down both sides, had its nose bashed in when some idiot pulled out of a side road in front of me, and got booted up the backside at a set of traffic lights. I have nothing against Fords, but I was particularly glad to see the back of that car.

Altogether there are four sets of valets in the country. I cover the area from Uttoxeter southwards, including the West Country, together with a valet called Robin Lord. There is another valet who does the Midlands, from Uttoxeter northwards as far as Nottingham, and after Nottingham the northern valets take over. Of course, we all have our own jockeys, so I go to places like Aintree and Doncaster and Haydock for the big northern meetings, and likewise the northern valets always come down to meetings like the Cheltenham Festival. We also have some 'second' jockeys, so that if someone like Graham Bradley or Jonjo, when he was riding, comes down to a lesser southern meeting I will look after him, but he carries all his own tack for that event. Nowadays, with better horses in the North than there used to be, northern horses and jockeys come South more often, and southern-based jockeys sometimes go up to meetings at places like Newcastle. With all these comings and goings it is a miracle that everyone's tack ends up in the right place day after day!

Apart from getting out of bed at the crack of dawn on a freezing winter morning, the one part of the job that I don't particularly enjoy is the bookkeeping, and fortunately Ann does all this for me. Now that I don't have to ask jockeys to pay up on the spot so that I can buy my petrol home, we send out bills on a monthly basis. Our charges are fixed in agreement with the Jockeys' Association and work on a sliding scale, but basically we are paid 10% of the jockey's riding fee, with VAT on top of that. When I first started valeting the fee for one ride was £1.10s. Still, in those days a jockey's riding fee was £15 — now it's nearer £50.

Once or twice a year we go to mixed meetings, for example the Whitbread at Sandown in April where all the other races on the card are on the flat. At times like this I'm extremely thankful that I'm involved in jump racing, because the flat jockeys are so serious. No larking about or telling jokes for them: between races they sit on the bench with their arms folded, chins on their chests, brows furrowed. Perhaps they're worrying about how to invest the odd half-million or two, but whatever it is, if that's what riches bring, they can keep it. Over the years I have seen some of the top flat-race jockeys undergo a tremendous change since the time they were apprentices, whereas someone like Steve Smith Eccles hasn't changed a bit from the day he first walked into a weighing room. Weighing room attendants will back this up, because they always say how pleased they are to see the jump jockeys back in August.

When I retired from race-riding one or two newspapers published articles which said that becoming a valet was something of a come-down, but I would not agree with that. It may be less glamorous than turning to training, but it is more secure and with fewer headaches. It is a great deal better than the fate that has befallen one or two jockeys I know, who are either doing factory jobs, or have invested money in ill-advised business ventures. I am happiest when I am among racing folk, and my job has enabled me to keep in touch with the game, and at the same time gives me a good living. Above all, I'm still in the jockeys' room, the holy of holies, from which even trainers are barred. In racing, it is quite simply the best place to be.

4

A DAY AT THE RACES

Sometimes of a freezing January morning, when the alarm rings at five o'clock, it's pitch black outside with frost on the ground and ice on the road, I think how pleasant it would be to turn over and go back to sleep in my warm bed for another couple of hours. But if I did that, not only would I lose my job, but if I was doing a meeting on my own there would be no racing at the course that day. This is because I carry in my car the boots, breeches, saddles, breastgirths, weightcloths and most of the other tack for the majority of the jockeys due to ride. The thought of being pursued not only by those jockeys, but by the Jockey Club, the Jockeys' Association and a few thousand irate punters is enough to get anyone out of bed.

Of course, I don't have to make a 5 a.m. start every day of the season, and the time I get up depends on how far I have to go. I like to be on the course about three hours before the first race, and I also allow time for a breakfast stop and for breakdowns, so if the first race is at Plumpton at noon it's a very early start indeed.

During the busy months of the season Tom and I plan our itineraries well in advance. Our commitments might involve a total of up to 3,000 miles' driving in six days and we try to split it as near to fifty/fifty as possible. A typical week in late November might see me going to Folkestone on the Monday — a round trip of over 350 miles, while

Tom goes up the road to Warwick. The following day I'll go to Huntingdon, about 140 miles there and back, and Tom does Newton Abbot. On the Wednesday and Thursday I'll do Plumpton and Wincanton, both long trips, and Tom will do Ludlow and Warwick again. On the Friday I go to Sandown for a two-day meeting, which means I stay overnight, while Tom has to flog up to Leicester and then all the way to Chepstow the following day. We usually manage to even things up. Most evenings we have to meet to swap tack, depending on where each jockey is going the following day; and if I'm doing the same meeting two days running but one of my jockeys isn't, I have to make sure that the jockey goes off with all his own tack at the end of the first day. I don't mind the travelling, apart from idiot drivers, but I sometimes wonder what the people who arrange the racing calendar are thinking about when they have us going to Folkestone one day, then all the way to the West Country for Newton Abbot or Devon and Exeter the following day, and then back to the South-east for Plumpton the day after that!

My car is loaded up the night before, and in the morning I creep out of the house as quietly as possible to avoid waking my wife and two daughters. I will either make my way straight to the course — if I'm on my own — or I'll drive over to Kineton to pick up my assistant, Andrew Townsend, a super fellow and a very good valet, but I wish to hell he'd learn to drive so that I didn't have to make a half-hour detour to pick him up some mornings!

We always stop for breakfast, usually at the same places, because we don't get much chance to eat during the day. One morning my brother and I were hammering down the M5 to Devon and Exeter when we heard on the radio that racing was off, so we decided to stop for breakfast at the next service area and then turn round and head home.

' . . . .And if there's any nonsense from you young claimers, you'll hear about it from me!' Taking stock of things in the weighing room.

As we got out of the car we saw two stable lads who we knew were on their way to the same meeting, so we told them not to bother. They thanked us for the information and went off to their horsebox. Tom and I had our breakfast, got back on the motorway, turned round at the next interchange and headed north. As we passed Gloucester we heard on the radio that the earlier report had been a hoax, and that racing would in fact go ahead. I was furious as I turned round yet again and drove flat-out to the course. When we got there, nearly an hour later than we should have done, the first people we saw were the two lads we had told to go home.

'How did you know racing was on?' I asked them.

'We heard it on the radio when we were leaving the service area,' they said.

I was so cross that it never occurred to me to ask them why the hell they hadn't thought to come back and tell Tom and me!

It can be very annoying when the weather is bad and you have to leave home at 6 a.m. knowing that it is highly likely that racing will be called off after a 7.30 inspection. I can ring the groundsman at the course, and he might tell me there's no chance, but I still have to rely on the official announcement after the stewards' inspection, so I have to be there on the spot. Life was a little easier in that respect when Terry Wogan used to have his morning show on Radio 2, because every day he tipped a 'Wogan's Winner', and he would always announce early in the day when racing was off.

When I arrive on the course the place is virtually deserted, only the Clerk of the Course and the head groundsman are about. Sometimes it's really quite eerie, especially on an occasion like Gold Cup day when the mist is hanging low over the course, and you can barely discern a few horses being exercised over the gallops, yet you know that in a few hours' time forty thousand people will be milling about the place.

I unload the car and sort out and hang up the tack. Each

jockey has his own peg. If the previous day's racing has been muddy, the boots and saddles will have been scrubbed and left to dry overnight, so they will all need polishing. I study the racecard to see what weight each of my jockeys has got in each race, in order to determine what size saddles he will need, and what weightcloths. Most of the top jockeys leave all their tack with me, so that they're only carrying their own helmets and back protectors. As well as the jockeys' own kit, I also carry around fifteen pairs of breeches, boots, saddles, gloves, tights, chafing pads, towels, whither pads and whips, and numerous other bits and pieces, so that I'm equipped to do running repairs to things like breeches buttons if necessary. When a young jockey comes into the weighing room for the first time he may not have all his own kit, so he'll borrow some from me, and I like to make sure that these youngsters are smartly turned out for their first rides. Apart from anything else, it creates a good impression with the owner and trainer.

Sometimes my own tack ends up in odd places. Usually the jockeys who borrow it return it by the end of the season, but occasionally they forget. Last summer Richard Rowe was riding at the Groenendaal track in Brussels for the British Jump Jockeys' team, and he must have been so anxious to get to the party afterwards that he left his bag in the weighing room. The item on the top of the bag, I'm not sure exactly what it was, had the name J. Buckingham written on it, and any ordinary Belgian jockey or valet seeing that would have no idea whose it was. Fortunately, the person who spotted the bag was Philippe Caus, the Belgian jockey who has ridden over here for Richard's guv'nor, Josh Gifford, so he knew who to return it to. Lucky for Rosie too, or he would have had a fat bill from the mysterious J. Buckingham.

While we are sorting out the kit, the weighing room gradually comes to life as all the other characters who make up the jigsaw appear on the scene — the tea man, the Clerk of the Scales, the announcers, head lads, trainers and

Humping saddles and polishing boots at Sandown in 1986.

so on. Most trainers or head lads will stick their heads round the weighing room door to remind me about a breastplate or blinkers for a certain horse, and I make sure that my card is marked accordingly. The trainers are responsible for the colours, and they deliver them to the weighing room door in good time so that I can hang them up with the rest of a jockey's kit. Most trainers are very good about looking after their colours, although there are one or two who have obviously yet to learn about the invention of the washing machine, or even soap! John Jenkins, on the other hand, always delivers his colours in spotless condition, wrapped in those cellophane bags that laundries use. Sometimes trainers forget to collect their colours at the end of the day: I once had a call from one who asked me if I had picked his up.

'Probably,' I said. 'Who was riding and where did you leave them?'

He told me, and I replied 'Sorry, I wasn't at that meeting.'

'Oh, it wasn't at the meeting last week,' he said, 'It was twelve months ago!'

The jockeys themselves begin to arrive an hour before their first race, some a bit earlier, some at the last minute. When he was riding, Bill Smith was always the first into the weighing room. 'All successful people are early,' he would say, and since he has followed a successful career in the saddle with an equally successful one as television pundit and adviser to the Racecourse Association, I reckon he has a fair point.

Things really start to hum once the jockeys are in and we're getting them ready for the first race. Apart from making sure that they're all prepared for the Clerk of the Scales I have to remember some of their individual foibles and superstitions. Graham Thorner, for instance, always used to get someone else to break in a new pair of breeches or a new saddle for him. He would even jump up and down on a new set of colours before putting them on. Others are superstitious about the colour green and won't use a green pad, which is all very well provided they don't tell me at the last minute so that I've got to rush around looking for another one. Peter Scudamore, when he first started to ride, was rather moody, although he's changed a great deal. Other jockeys' moods will depend on the quality of their rides, and I have to remember that sometimes a jockey is under tremendous pressure from an owner or trainer, and if things don't go right for him it might affect his future rides. Steve Smith Eccles is quite demanding: he has a certain routine for getting dressed, and when he's got his gloves on he'll come over and say 'Put a band on there, please,' and even if you're busy sorting out someone else he'll hover over you until you attend to him, which increases the pressure. When it comes to looking after jockeys I don't differentiate between a top rider, like Steve, or a young claimer — they all pay me the same money — but I do like to get Steve done and out of the way as early as possible. Fortunately, he's always one of the first into the weighing room, and despite his demands the place would be a lot duller without him.

Once the jockeys have arrived we're flat out until after the last race, with barely time for a cup of tea. When they go out for the first race we start to get their kit ready for the next, which means putting up the next set of colours and changing the saddle to a lighter or heavier one if necessary. This can be a very hectic time, especially on busy days like Bank holidays when there might be seven or eight meetings, and each of those has about ninety runners and only thirty jockeys. Also, there is only half an hour between races, so if you have a three-mile chase on the card the actual changing time between the end of that race and going out into the parade ring for the next one is negligible.

It's on such occasions that you have to make sure that the jockeys don't start fussing about being ready in time, because that just creates more pressure. If a new young jockey looks the panicking type, we try to get it out of his system as early as possible. Hywel Davies was bad at first, but he's all right now. David Nicholson always panicked. 'Come on, come on, get a move on!', he used to say, and in the end we would both be flapping like mad and nothing got done. John Francome, on the other hand, was brilliant. He never, ever, made a fuss. He would just stand there cool and calm and wait his turn. If every jockey was like him, my job would be bliss.

Apart from the routine of getting all the jockeys ready to ride there are usually plenty of other things going on in the weighing room. Anything, from watching Steve Smith Eccles pull off one of his practical jokes on an unsuspecting newcomer, to getting a message to an injured jockey's wife, or arranging for someone else to take his car home. I have even had stable lads borrow a fiver off me to get diesel for the horsebox on the return journey because their guv'nor has forgotten to do it. At Sandown once, I was called out to help a trainer's wife glue a broken fingernail back on, and there was an occasion when someone sent a message into the weighing room saying that his girlfriend was cold and could I please cut the legs off a pair of tights to make some knickers for her. Presumably she had expected warmer weather and had dressed, or rather not dressed, accordingly!

After the last race the jockeys shower and change, grab a sandwich and a cup of tea, and then get going. The last jockey to leave is usually Peter Scudamore, who is one of the slowest people I have ever come across in the weighing room. Before they all go, they tell me where they are racing the following day, or in some cases in three days' time, so that I know whether I need to take their kit with me or pass it on to my brother if we're doing separate meetings.

At this stage of the day, with the jockeys on their way home and the punters celebrating, or drowning their sorrows, in the racecourse bars, we valets still have plenty of work to do. All the kit has to be cleaned — saddles and boots washed and polished, girths scrubbed, breeches into the washing machine. Fortunately, all the courses have washing machines and tumble driers in the weighing rooms these days which makes life a lot easier, especially after a really muddy day, when sometimes I can't recognise the jockeys as they come in after a race. Once, after a particularly mucky day, I left Folkestone just after ten o'clock at night and met my brother in Banbury at 1 a.m. to swap kit from one car to the other. I also got locked in at Ascot once, when they said they wanted me out by seven o'clock. I had told them 8.30 p.m. at the earliest but no one seemed to have taken any notice — Ascot is that kind of place.

No matter what time I leave a course, or what time I get home, I still get up at five o'clock the next morning if I have to, because if I didn't, there might be no racing....

5

SECRETS OF THE
WEIGHING ROOM

Anyone putting his head round the weighing room door during racing would encounter a scene that appeared to be pure chaos. Jockeys, trainers, travelling head lads and officials are all milling about, shouting instructions and messages, with everybody going in different directions. In actual fact, things are following an established and well-organised pattern which ensures that racing proceeds smoothly and on schedule — and according to the rules. Before we get on to some of the more amusing and scurrilous goings-on in the weighing room, it is worth explaining the formal procedures which take place before and after each race.

To begin with, the term 'weighing room' does not just refer to the area where the jockeys change. It is actually a complex of rooms consisting of the outer area, where the scales are; the jockeys' changing room, where no one other than jockeys and valets is allowed; the stewards' room; the secretary's office and the ambulance room, which is usually behind the jockeys' changing room.

The man who presides over the weighing room is the Clerk of the Scales. His is one of the most important and responsible jobs on the racecourse, involving a great deal of attention to detail and assembling of information, as well as ensuring that every jockey in every race weighs out and weighs in correctly. The Clerk of the Scales will be at his desk in front of the scales themselves about two hours before racing starts. He remains there until every jockey has weighed in after the last race, often spending five hours or so bundled up in sweaters and overcoats in a cold, draughty weighing room.

The runners for each race are declared at the overnight stage, which means in fact that they must be declared by noon on the previous day. Any trainer withdrawing a horse after that will be in trouble unless he can provide a vet's certificate with a good reason. When the travelling head lad arrives at the course he (or she) will formally declare all the horses in his charge to the Declarations Clerks.

The Declarations Clerks will pass this information on to the Clerk of the Scales, together with details of blinkers which are declared at the overnight stage, and will also inform us valets of any non-runners.

The travelling head lad will tell the valets about any extras that his horses are carrying, and we note this information in our racecard, so that all our jockeys will have the correct tack for each race. Apart from the extras we also have to ensure that the jockey has the correct saddle, since there are three different weights of saddle, ranging from 2 lb to 6 lb. The trainer himself is responsible for the jockey's colours, which he brings to the weighing room prior to racing. Forgetting to bring them, or bringing the wrong ones, results in a fine.

Once a jockey is fully dressed for a race we give him his tack and he gets on to a set of scales in the jockeys' changing room itself, which we call try-scales. This is for us to make sure that he has the correct weight and that we have not omitted anything. The trainer will then come to the weighing room and call his jockey out. The jockey collects his number cloth from a man by the door, and

A recent picture of me, standing besides the try-scales in the jockeys' changing room.

then gets on the proper scales to formally weigh out in front of the Clerk of the Scales, whom, incidentally, he calls 'Sir'. He tells him his number and the weight he is supposed to be doing, as well as informing him of any extra tack, such as a breastplate or breastgirth. The only equipment that the jockey does not carry when weighing out is his helmet and his whip. The Clerk of the Scales notes all the details on sheets of paper: it is his responsibility to ensure that every jockey has the correct weight, number and colours. He has other responsibilities too, such as giving permission for any message or information to be broadcast on the course's public address system.

Having weighed out, the jockey hands his equipment to his trainer or the travelling head lad, who will then go and tack up the horse. The jockey himself returns to the jockeys' room. If a jockey is not riding in one race he can do all this at leisure while that race takes place. If he has three or four races on the trot his life is a little more hectic. Hence the scenes of apparent chaos in the weighing room.

About fifteen minutes before each race the doorman, whose job it is to prevent unauthorised persons coming into the jockeys' room, calls out 'Jockeys, get ready!', and five minutes later he will call 'Jockeys, out!', and the jockeys will leave the weighing room to go to the parade ring.

When the jockeys return to the weighing room after a race the first four finishers have to weigh in, and the rest may or may not, at the discretion of the Clerk of the Scales. Jockeys never know in advance whether or not they will all have to weigh in, so as they come into the weighing room the unplaced ones will call out 'All weigh, sir?' The object of the weigh-in is, of course, to make sure that every jockey comes back with all the equipment he went out with, and is at the correct weight. Any jockey who is 2 lb over or 1 lb underweight at the weigh-in is disqualified, and will come up in front of the stewards.

It is at the weigh-in, also, that objections and stewards enquiries are dealt with. If the stewards decide to hold an enquiry into the running of a horse or the riding tactics of a jockey, they have to decide on this very quickly after the end of the race and inform the Clerk of the Scales of their decision. This information is broadcast on the public address system, so that punters know to hold on to all betting slips until the result of the enquiry is known. This is particularly important if the horse you backed to win was placed second but the placings are subsequently reversed!

If one jockey objects to another, for things like bumping or taking his ground, he must register his objection when he weighs in. The Clerk of the Scales notes this and the jockey must fill in a form listing the name of the jockey he is objecting to and the reason. The stewards then take over and the jockeys concerned are called into the stewards' room to be interviewed; as well as that the stewards will study a video film of the incident. It costs a jockey £40 to register an objection, and he will lose his money if the objection is found by the stewards to be without grounds.

Once all the jockeys have weighed in, and the Clerk of the Scales has noted that they have done the correct weight and that their equipment is in order, the paperwork for that race is set aside. Eventually it goes to Wetherbys, who deal with all jockeys' accounts, so that they can work out how much each jockey is due in riding fees, percentages and so on at the end of the day.

I don't think that anyone in racing would deny that jockeys do the odd bit of fiddling from time to time in order to make the weight. 'Cheating' is too strong a word to use, because no one goes as far as to try to prevent their own horse from winning or to prevent another horse from beating it. The jockeys simply use the odd ruse to weigh out and weigh back in at the correct weight, when they would be 2 lb or 3 lb overweight if they were carrying everything they were supposed to be carrying.

One jockey, who rode at the same time as I did, had weak wrists, so he wore wrist supports which were made of leather and which had iron strips inside them to keep his wrists steady during the race. These supports must have weighed nearly 1 lb each, and when you're struggling to do a low weight every ounce counts. Anyway, I was standing in the weighing room one day as the jockeys came back to weigh in, when suddenly this pair of wrist supports came flying through the open window.. The jockey had weighed out without them, worn them to ride, and needed to get rid of them again before he weighed in.

A few years ago I saw an incident when a jockey returned to the scales and was found to be 3 lb under-weight. I don't know how he managed it, and I don't think he did either, but it was a serious situation for him because he had been first past the post and now he was about to lose the race through a disqualification.

As soon as the Clerk of the Scales pointed this out, a jockey who was unplaced, standing behind the winner, immediately dropped a pad, picked it up and handed it to our man sweating on the scales, with the words 'You must have dropped this.' Holding the pad, the jockey made the correct weight and kept the race. It was a piece of very quick thinking, if slightly risky, and it just goes to illustrate the camaraderie that exists between jump jockeys.

Having related these two stories, I should stress that they are very minor incidents, that they don't happen every day, and that the Clerks of the Scales are no mugs. They work under a lot of pressure, especially at meetings where there are big fields and a lot of jockeys have to weigh in and weigh out quickly. They cannot be expected to spot everything, but neither do they miss a lot. One jockey I know once weighed out wearing a pair of 'cheating boots', which are boots made of very thin leather, weighing next to nothing, and which are then changed for the real thing before the jockey goes out to ride. As this particular jockey left the scales, however, the Clerk of the Scales stopped him and said, 'I trust you're going to ride in *those* boots?' The jockey had no option but to do so.

Actually, I think that most of the minor fiddling which goes on would not be necessary if the authorities raised the minimum riding weight from 10 stone to 10 stone 7. That would still leave a 2 stone difference between top and bottom weight and the only people affected would be the young claimers, who these days get plenty of rides anyway (I did a meeting at Plumpton recently where more than half the jockeys were claimers). Having been around the weighing room for thirty years, I am convinced that today's lads are generally bigger than jockeys were when I started riding, probably because today's diets are better than those of the 1950s.

Nowadays more and more top jump jockeys, reaching their prime around the age of thirty, are beginning to struggle with their weight and are having to go through some dreadful deprivations to keep it down, just at a time when they have done all the hard work and ought to be reaping the rewards. Hywel Davies, for example, is one of our top jockeys, but he is quite tall and he seems to live on fresh air and spend all his spare time in the sauna. He usually looks like death warmed up. Graham Bradley is reckoned by many to be one of the most stylish jockeys in the business, but because he can't do the lower weights he misses quite a few rides. If Brad could make 10 stone, I am sure he would have been well in contention for the jockeys' championship for the last few years.

So a bit of fiddling goes on from time to time, but nothing very serious. All in all, I reckon that the Clerks of the Scales and all the other officials at our racecourses do a very good job. The Clerk of the Course has to worry about everything from organising an early-morning inspection if there is frost about, to sorting things out if one of our washing machines breaks down, and he and the racecourse manager have a million and one things to worry about during a meeting. When you think about it that way, it makes looking after twenty or thirty jockeys sound like very small beer.

6

TALES FROM THE WEIGHING ROOM

If things aren't buzzing in the weighing room, they aren't buzzing at all. Myself, quoted in *The Sporting Life*

The weighing room is the jockeys' sanctuary amidst the hurly-burly of the racecourse. Apart from the valets, no one else is allowed into the jockeys' room. It is almost a sacred place if you like — a place of great elation and sometimes deep despair; a place to relax, have a cup of tea, read the paper, think about the next race, chat with your mates. But despite the serious business of racing, life in the weighing room is never dull, and whatever else is going on the jockeys' sense of humour is never far from the surface.

I have come across a lot of weighing room characters in the past thirty years, but one who was always cracking jokes, or pulling a stunt at someone else's expense, was John Francome, a brilliant jockey and equally brilliant wit. John has an instant sense of humour, and could bring the house down with one remark.

A few years ago Jimmy Hill was riding in a charity race at Sandown Park. He phoned me a day or so before the race to ask if I could fit him up with a pair of size eleven boots. I joked with him, saying I supplied jockeys, not navvies, and I mentioned this to John Francome next time I saw him. Straight away, John replied 'I wouldn't worry about the boots Buck. Your big problem is going to be his chinstrap!'

On another occasion John was sitting in the weighing room at Folkestone, waiting to see the doctor. (If a jockey is injured in a fall, he gets a red entry in his medical book, and he's not allowed to ride again until he gets a black one.) John had arrived early to get his black entry, but the doctor wasn't there, so he left a message to say he was in the weighing room, and started getting ready to ride. A little later, when the weighing room was full of jockeys, a door at the far end opened and an elderly chap appeared, stooping a bit and walking with a stick. 'John Francome?' he enquired.

'Over here,' shouted John from the other end of the room.

The old fellow began to hobble over to John. 'I hear you want to see a doctor,' he said.

'No disrespect sir,' replied John 'But you look as though you could do with seeing one yourself.'

Everyone in the weighing room collapsed with a great roar of laughter, and I felt quite sorry for the old duffer.

John's big mate in the weighing room was Steve Smith Eccles, and I know that Steve misses his company a great deal now that John has retired. Steve is frequently referred to as the last of the cavalier jockeys, and in many ways he and John are quite different. Steve enjoys a party and a good night out, whereas John, if you can get him to come to the party at all, will usually be one of the first to leave. Steve also enjoys a drink from time to time, whereas John hardly drinks at all. And yet they are great friends, even going on holiday together, and I think this has a lot to do with their shared sense of fun.

They both used to enjoy a good practical joke at someone else's expense, and a few years ago I watched them pull a particularly dirty trick on Andy Turnell.

Nowadays, this joke is well known on the circuit, but it originated in the North and at the time none of the southern jockeys knew about it. Anyway, John and Steve came into the weighing room one day, and as they dumped their kit I noticed Steve wink at John and say he was off next door to get a cup of tea. I knew straight away that something was up so I waited to see what would happen.

When Steve had gone out, John went up to Andy Turnell. 'Hey Andy,' he said. 'When Steve comes back, ask him about his mum's piano playing.'

'His what?' asked Andy.

'Well, you see, his mum plays the piano and she's just won a competition and she's very proud about it. She keeps telling all her friends but Steve finds it quite embarrassing. Go on, ask him about it when he comes back in.'

'Okay,' said Andy.

So when Steve came back with his cup of tea Andy piped up 'Hey, Steve, what's all this about your mum playing the piano?'

'What d'you mean?' said Steve.

'Well, you know. I hear she's a bit good on the ivories. Won a competition didn't she?'

Steve walked up to Andy and looked him straight in the eye. 'My mum's got no hands,' he said.

Andy's face was a picture! If ever a man wanted the floor to open up for him, Andy Turnell did then. I thought he was going to burst into tears, but John and Steve couldn't contain themselves any longer, they burst out laughing, and Andy took the joke in good part.

Some jockeys react differently to the same stunt. I remember that it fell rather flat when someone tried it on Bob Champion. When the chap said 'My mum's got no hands,' Bob just replied 'Oh, hasn't she?', and carried on getting dressed. On another occasion John and Steve tried it out on a new young jockey called Jeff Kerr. After Steve had delivered the punch line, Jeff Kerr looked puzzled and

There weren't many occasions when John Francome didn't have a smile on his face and a joke to tell. Here he is, mop-headed, boyish looking, in front of the scales at Cheltenham, with that great Irish jockey Frank Berry.

scratched his head for a moment. Then he said 'How the bloody hell did she manage to win a piano competition if she's got no hands?'

John even enjoys having a laugh at his best friend's expense, and I saw him upset Steve one day at Newbury. It all started when Steve came into the weighing room looking hot and bothered after being beaten a length into second place.

'You should have won that race Eck,' said John.

'How?'

'You should have held him up. The horse needs holding up. If you'd held him up you'd have won.'

'Well why the bloody hell didn't you tell me that before the race?' exploded Steve.

'You didn't ask me,' John replied.

Some of John's jokes have also been known to give serious cause for alarm. Two or three years ago he was travelling to America with the British Jump Jockeys' team to ride at Fair Hill in Maryland. As the plane took off from Gatwick and lumbered into the sky, John asked what make it was.

'A DC10,' someone said.

'Oh, I know,' John said in a loud voice. 'These are the planes that are always crashing.' Several people sitting near him, including Jonjo O'Neill, turned white, and there was a sudden rush for the toilet!

One day John drove Nicky Henderson and another jockey down to a meeting in the West Country. He had four or five rides and on the motorway coming back he said he was tired, and asked if anyone else would like to drive. No one replied, so John put the car into cruise-control and climbed calmly into the back seat for a sleep, leaving a startled Nicky Henderson to grab the wheel and steer from the front passenger seat. Any policeman passing at that moment would have seen a BMW steaming up the motorway at probably a good deal more than 70 miles per hour, with two people in the back seat, a wide-eyed front-seat passenger, and no driver!

The worst stunt I ever saw John Francome pull was in the old weighing room at Kempton Park. In the toilets there John discovered some yellow blocks of disinfectant, quite worn and looking exactly like pineapple chunks. Francome immediately saw the potential in these blocks, so he gathered them all up, put them in a bag, and went round offering them to the other jockeys. But the jockeys were suspicious, because it wasn't like John to be so generous with sweets, and sensibly they all refused. So John left the bag on the table close to the door.

The fellow on duty at the door had been watching all this, and his mouth was watering. He couldn't reach the bag from where he was standing, so he began inching closer and closer to the table, looking furtively around the room to make sure no one had noticed. Of course the whole weighing room was watching him, although everybody pretended to be doing something else. Eventually he got close enough to reach the bag, and he took one of the delicious-looking 'sweets' and popped it into his mouth. In a flash he realised what it was, spat it out, let out a roar of alarm and took off. We didn't see him again that day!

One day Francome, Hywel Davies and a couple of other jockeys shared a car to Ludlow. On the way home they stopped near Gloucester for petrol and all of them went into the garage shop. Hywel came out with a coke, and as they drove away said 'Cheers, whoever bought the coke.'

'Wasn't me,' said John, and none of the others had paid for it either. Oh well, thought Hywel, I've got a free coke.

When John arrived home some friends were there and he got one of them to telephone Hywel.

'Mr Davies?'

'Yes.'

'Mr Davies, this is Chief Constable Jones from the Gloucestershire Constabulary. Were you at a certain garage outside Gloucester at about half past four this afternoon?'

'Yes, I was,' said Hywel.

'And do you realise that while you were there you stole a can of Coke from the garage shop?'

'Oh!' said Hywel, starting to flap. 'Oh, Good God! What shall I do?'

'We have a lot of this happening in the Gloucester area, Mr Davies,' went on the imposter. 'And it's just not on.

Unless you can give me an explanation for your behaviour, I shall have to consider taking action.'

'Oh dear,' said Hywel, thinking fast and sounding more Welsh by the minute. 'Well look, I'll tell you what I'll do. I'm going back that way tomorrow and I'll stop and pay for it then.'

By this stage poor old Hywel was getting into quite a sweat about the whole business, and it was only when Francome and his friends burst into laughter that he realised he'd been had.

Hywel is a super bloke and everyone likes him a lot, even when he forgets things. Every year some of the top jockeys give the valets a bottle of something at Christmas and every year Hywel asks us what sort of whisky we'd like — but we're still waiting for it! It's becoming something of a joke in the weighing room now. 'When are you going to the off-licence, Hywel?' 'Hey, Hywel, tell Rachel to put three bottles of Scotch on her shopping list next week.' As Hywel left the weighing room at the end of last season, he shouted 'See you in August, Buck. Hey, I still owe you that whisky!'

A few years ago Hywel took the most terrible fall at Doncaster. A lot of people will remember it because it was a televised race. It was a real pile-driver of a fall, and in fact Hywel stopped breathing in the ambulance and had to be resuscitated. The mood in the weighing room was sombre for once.

That same day someone had brought a new pair of boots into the weighing room. They were made with a much stiffer material than the usual riding boots, and, in fact, they looked more like jackboots. No one was very impressed with them and someone stood them upside down — the material was that stiff — in the middle of the weighing room floor.

A little while later, word came through that Hywel had recovered consciousness and was going to be all right. Everyone was mightily relieved and some joker, who had better be nameless on this occasion, went over to the pair of boots, bent down, and shouted 'Okay Hywel, you can come out now!'

★   ★   ★

The weighing room was just as much fun in the days when I was riding myself — we also had our comedians and practical jokers. People like Roy Mangan, who came back to the weighing room one day with his helmet on back-to-front. 'Crikey,' he said. 'You should have seen my fella whip round at the start!' Roy's favourite party trick was to cut the crotches in people's underpants, so that when they pulled them on — often standing on a chair to avoid the wet floor — they looked right idiots as the underpants went up to their armpits!

David Sunderland was another funny man. At Southwell one day his horse fell out in the country, and as he walked back in he took some gorse from one of the hurdles and stuffed it inside his helmet. When he got back to the weighing room he chucked the helmet on the table, exclaiming 'Bloody hell! That bugger didn't jump very high!'

Actually, David Sunderland was the perpetrator of one inadvertent escapade which is very amusing in retrospect but was not so funny at the time. David lived quite near me, outside Banbury, and one evening he rang up to ask for a lift to Plumpton on the following day. In those days I used to go to all the southern meetings by train, so I suggested that he meet me at Banbury station the next morning, and we could travel down together. 'That's no good,' he said. 'I have to ride out tomorrow morning and it'll be too late to go by train by the time I finish.'

So I agreed to drive, but I told David he would have to navigate, because I'd never been to Plumpton by car before.

'That's no problem,' he said. 'I've driven there many times.'

I picked him up the next morning and off we went. In

those days, of course, there was no M23 or M25 and, once we got south of London, David was navigating by memory. He seemed to have everything under control. 'Oh, yes,' he said. 'That's the garage where we stopped for petrol last time. That's the pub where we had a drink on the way back. That's the gate where we stopped for a piss.' On and on he went, recognising landmarks all over the place.

I was just thinking about congratulating him on his efforts, when we drew up outside the gates of Fontwell Park!

To say I was not best pleased is an understatement, and the atmosphere in the car was pretty thick as we dashed over to Plumpton. Anyway, David got his just desserts for incompetent map-reading because I arrived in time for all my rides, but he had missed his first one, and the stewards fined him £10.

David was lucky not to get arrested at Plumpton on another occasion, although his offence was in any case through no fault of his own. The old weighing room there had narrow windows at head height. David had taken off his riding kit and was walking over to the showers, naked as the day he was born, when a couple of us grabbed him and held him up at the windows so that anyone passing by would have had a very good view of his 'three-piece suite'. We then walked along the side of the weighing room from one end to the other, with David in this predicament. As it happened, the only person passing at the time was a woman police constable. She performed a sharp eyes right towards the offending sight, and remained transfixed as she walked the length of the weighing room wall. Obviously she was most impressed with what she saw, although she didn't go as far as doing an about-turn and walking back for a second look!

Another riding contemporary of mine was Philip Blacker, who of course is now an exceptionally talented equine sculptor. Phil had a lovely dry, quiet sense of humour which sometimes made a pleasant change from some of our more raucous goings-on. Phil was riding at Hereford one day, and he and Roy Mangan were right at the back of the field on two no-hopers, virtually tailed-off. Roy was obviously getting frustrated because about three fences from home he picked up his stick and gave his horse a few taps, not that it would have made any difference, but Roy just wanted to point out who was in charge.

At this point Phil Blacker came upsides him and said 'Don't you think you're being a little optimistic Roy?'

One of the noisiest characters of the weighing room in my days as a jockey was Martin Blackshaw. Blackie was a northern-based jockey but he rode a lot in the South. He was a bouncy, brash fellow, a big practical joker who was disliked by a lot of jockeys, although I got on very well with him. Most of us fell victim to one of his pranks sooner or later, but we drew the line when he started going round asking if he could hypnotise us. 'Go on,' he said. 'You let me hypnotise you, and I'll prove to you that when I ask you to do something, you won't be able to do it.' At first nobody would take him on and Blackie spent months trying to get someone to agree.

Finally he persuaded an innocent young claimer in the weighing room at Southwell. He told the lad to stand to attention and close his eyes. Then he took him by the elbows and lowered him to the floor. 'Now keep your eyes closed,' he said. 'And when I give you a command, you won't be able to do it.' With that Blackie dropped his trousers and squatted over the fellow's face. 'Now sit up!' he ordered!

All the jockeys were determined to get their revenge on Blackie, and Ron Atkins and I worked out a plan. It was based on a party game in which you make a funnel with a piece of newspaper, stick the narrow end in your trousers, then put a penny coin on your forehead and try to drop it down the funnel. One day at Devon and Exeter Ron and I made a funnel and were pretending to argue about it when Blackie came in.

'I know I can do this,' I was saying.

'And I bet you can't,' replied Ron.

'What's all this?' demanded Blackie.

'Ron says I can't drop this penny off my forehead into this funnel.'

'Give it here,' said Blackie, who always liked to be in the limelight.

So we gave him the funnel and he stuck it into his trousers, and as he tilted his head back to balance the penny we poured a glass of water down the funnel. Blackie was furious and chased me all round the weighing room, but it was sweet revenge after all his pranks.

Another good friend of mine at that time was the jockey Neil Kernick, who was based in the West Country. Neil had a terrible stutter, so of course he was the butt of quite a few jokes, though he always took them in good part. Johnny Williams also had a stutter and the other jockeys used to ask the two of them what they talked about when they rang each other up. Neil's stutter was so bad sometimes that when he picked up the telephone he couldn't speak for ages. He once told me that if I telephoned him and I heard a whistling sound at the other end I wasn't to think I was going mad — it was Neil's way of letting people know he was there, otherwise they would ring off.

To try to get his voice going Neil would thump his chest with the palm of his hand, and occasionally he would also hop up and down. One day at Devon and Exeter I was having a wash and as I looked into the mirror I saw Neil going past in the direction of the toilets. Now when you see a jockey heading for the toilets just before he goes out to ride, you usually say 'Novice chasing, then?' So I called out 'Hey Neil, novice chasing, then?' Neil stopped for a moment and began to thump his chest violently, but this had no effect so he started to hop up and down as well. The last thing I saw was this little fellow thumping his chest and hopping off into the loo on one leg, with no sound at all coming out of his mouth!

Neil now trains a few horses in the West Country and I recently saw him at a meeting down there. I explained that

I was writing a book and that I intended to include this story. He said that it was fine and confirmed that I had got the details right. We watched a race from the stands and then Neil said goodbye and walked down to the exit at the bottom. Just before he disappeared from sight I noticed that he was looking up at me, and then he thumped his chest and hopped away on one leg. Lovely man!

Another lavatorial story concerns the old weighing room at Fontwell. The loo doors in this establishment had no locks on them, and when John Southern went in there one day he automatically propped his leg up against the door to secure himself from intruders. What he had forgotten was that the doors opened outwards, so that when someone came along and tried the door, there was John sitting on the loo reading the *Sporting Life*, with one leg stuck straight out in front of him for no apparent reason!

One day Roger Rowell was driving Gary Moore to Towcester. There was an accident on the main road which was holding them up so Roger headed off around the country lanes to try to avoid the jam. Gary Moore was struggling a bit with his weight at the time and had taken what we call a pee-pill. They are aptly nicknamed because they do make you want to pee, although they also have rather unpleasant dehydrating side effects.

Gary felt the pill doing its work so he asked Roger to stop. This was impossible, because not only were they running late, but there was also a queue of cars behind them and no convenient farm-gate or lane. Poor Gary was getting really desperate, so he tried to pee out of the car window but it just flew back in his face. Eventually he remembered the tube of Steradent which he carries around with him for his false teeth. He took all the pills out of that and peed into it, bailing it out every few seconds. I hope he remembered to wash it out before he replaced the pills!

At Lingfield once I noticed Gary's false teeth sitting in their glass of Steradent while he was out riding. They had a large sort of plate attached to them and that gave me an idea. I went next door to the tea-room and fetched some mustard which I then proceeded to smear all over the top of the plate. That done, I put the teeth back in the glass and waited. When Gary returned he automatically popped his teeth back in his mouth without looking, and two seconds later he hit the roof! I think some of the other jockeys thought for a minute he was having a fit. When he found out who the culprit was, he said to me 'I didn't mind the joke, Buck, it's just that I can't stand bloody mustard!'

Talking of mustard reminds me of a story about Sam Morshead. Sam is a well-bred Irishman — if there is such a thing — and like most Irishmen he has his eccentricities. One of these is the way in which he gets undressed. Instead of taking off each garment individually, Sam undoes the top three buttons of his shirt, loosens his tie, then removes the tie, shirt, sweater and vest all at once, hanging them in a bundle on his peg. He removes his underpants and trousers together as well, and I'm sure he would do the same with his shoes and socks if he could.

Anyway, one day Sam came back to the weighing room after a fall, from which he'd emerged unscathed except for a bleeding nose. When he came out of the shower his nose was still streaming blood so he made a tissue into a roll and stuck that up his nostril. Then he got himself a huge great doorstep of a ham sandwich, covered in mustard. With this snack in one hand and the tissue protruding from his nose, he then tried to get dressed. You can imagine the struggle he had, especially as he was attempting to put on three layers of clothing plus his tie at the same time. He made it after about twenty minutes' of contortions, and considerable laughter from the other jockeys. I asked him why he didn't just do it the simple way, but I don't think that had occurred to him!

These days there are a great many Irish jockeys in the weighing room. I have tried to avoid Irish jokes in this book because so many of them are old hat, but there are a couple which I can't resist repeating. The first, which I swear is true because I heard it with my own ears, concerns an Irish jockey who came into the weighing room last season looking as though he'd had a few days on the hard stuff. Sure enough, his first words were 'Bloody hell, I've been on the booze for five days now, and I can do 10 stone 1.'

'Well stay on it for one more day,' replied his mate. 'And you'll be able to do 10 stone.'

The second story, which may or may not be true, concerns a bunch of Irishmen who brought their car over on the ferry from Dublin to Liverpool for the Cheltenham Festival meeting. As they came down the M6 and into the Midlands, they spotted some roadsigns which displayed the letters HR in black lettering on a yellow background. They followed these and ended up in South Wales, unaware that HR stands for Holiday Route, not Horse Racing!

Every jockey finds himself hauled up in front of the stewards at some time in his career, but there was a time when John Francome seemed to be on the carpet virtually every day. I think it might have been something to do with his famous remark comparing stewards to 'cabbage-patch kids'!

He was changing at Plumpton one day when an attendant stuck his head around the door and called 'Francome! Stewards' room please!' John was stripped to the waist so he fished in his bag and pulled out a T-shirt which had the legend 'You're always alone with Herpes' printed on the front. That won't help you if you're in trouble, I thought, but John put it on and off he went. He came back about ten minutes later and everyone wanted to know what the problem was this time.

'What did the stewards say, John?' someone asked.

John looked down at the lettering on his T-shirt and shook his head. 'I don't think they even understand what it means,' he said.

And we never did find out what the trouble was.

As John has featured so much in this chapter, I think he should also have the last word. One year, a few days before Christmas, all the jockeys were talking about what sort of presents they had bought for their families. John, who is well known for being careful with his money, remarked 'I'm not going to buy my grandfather a present until Christmas Eve.'

'Why not?' someone asked.

'He might die,' John replied.

Anthony Webber piped up 'It's funny you should say that. I bought my grandfather a book one year, and blow me if he didn't die a few days later.'

'Well then,' said John in a deadpan voice. 'You ought to buy your grandmother a course in seances, then she can read it to him.'

TALES FROM
FAR PAVILIONS

During the 1960s David Nicholson, otherwise known as the Duke, formed the National Hunt jockeys' cricket team, which toured all over the country playing friendly games or charity matches on most weekends during the summer. Occasionally we used to go to Ireland or Jersey as well, and more recently the team has travelled as far afield as the West Indies. David, of course, appointed himself team captain, a position he still holds today, and other regulars in those early years included Jeff King, Terry Biddlecombe, Josh and Macer Gifford and myself. I was never very good at cricket, but I think they liked to have me around as an occasional bowler and team jester.

To say that the Duke's approach to life is a little competitive is to understate things slightly, and he took his cricket as seriously as he did his riding, and later his training. This was perfectly illustrated at the start of one season when a new LBW law had been introduced. Before the game began one of the umpires asked me if I was familiar with the new rule, and I replied that I wasn't absolutely sure but that I thought it meant the bowler's front foot could straddle the front popping crease, but must not cross it completely. The umpire seemed satis-

The National Hunt Jockeys' cricket team at Shanklin Cricket Ground during our 1968 tour of the Isle of Wight. Back row, left to right: Victor Dartnell, Jim Meads, Macer Gifford, David McCreary, Richard Tate, Jeff King, Butch Rumble, Dick Wellen. Front row, left to right: Richard Nicholson, David Nicholson, Josh Gifford, myself, Peter Devereaux, Tim Norman — winner of the National the year before me on Anglo. Some of our off-the-field pranks might not have been of a very high standard, but our cricketing gear certainly was, with our sweaters and caps of buff and gold — the Queen Mother's racing colours.

fied, and we went out to field. As usual the Duke had exercised his captain's prerogative and was opening the bowling. He didn't bother with a loosener first ball and, unconcerned about any new laws, he just came steaming in and gave it everything.

'No ball!' cried the umpire.

'Bollocks!' yelled back the Duke, quick as a flash.

He never allowed the umpire to get the upper hand.

We used to go to Ireland once a year to play a team organised by Victor McCalmont who owned the Mount Juliet Stud at Thomastown. It was a very good weekend: we arrived on the Saturday in time to watch the Irish Oaks, staying over in private accommodation where we were very well entertained, played cricket on the Sunday and flew back on the Monday morning.

The first year we went over we won the match easily, and when we came back the following year Victor had a much stronger team out. One of our opening batsmen was Gerald Dartnell, a very useful cricketer who could usually be relied upon to score 40 or 50, and on this occasion David Nicholson had stressed that much was expected of him.

I was sitting on the boundary with David when Gerald was given out LBW in the third over with only a few runs to his name. David immediately turned to me and said, 'That wasn't out, was it Buck?'

'I don't know, David,' I replied. 'I can't tell from this angle, can I?'

'Of course it wasn't out,' said David, getting to his feet. 'Get back in there!' he shouted to Gerald, who was making his way to the pavilion. 'That wasn't out. Oi! Umpire! That wasn't out!'

'Oh, sorry, David,' said the umpire, who had obviously been completely taken aback by this display of outrage. He let Gerald back in and Gerald went on to score quite a few, with the end result that we won the game. The opposition were very good about it and didn't complain, though I expect they all made a mental note not to tangle with the Duke at any level.

However, the Duke is certainly no ogre; he is a kind and considerate man who simply does not suffer fools gladly. I once broke my leg towards the end of the racing season, so instead of playing cricket that summer I was stuck at home with my leg in plaster from thigh to ankle, feeling sorry for myself. One weekend David kindly arranged for Anthony Webber to pick me up and drive me over to where the team was playing, not far away from my home. When I arrived at the ground David enquired solicitously after my health and asked me if I would like to do a little umpiring. I said that would be fine, so they provided me with a shooting stick and off I went. Because of the plaster on my leg I had to lean back on the shooting stick at quite a precarious angle, but it was good to be out on the field again, mixing with the team.

The opposition won the toss and batted. David opened the bowling at my end. The opening batsman was Jeremy Hindley, another very competent cricketer, whom our team would have been very glad to have seen back in the pavilion without too many runs to his name. In his second over David struck Jeremy on the pads and appealed massively for LBW. Not out, I said.

David was furious. He went bright red, strode back to his mark, knocking me off the shooting stick as he went, and refused to speak to me for the rest of the day, even during the tea interval. It was only in the bar afterwards, when we were all relaxing with a beer, that he approached me.

'OK then,' he said in a steely voice. 'Why didn't you give Hindley out?'

'The ball was missing leg stump,' I replied.

He gave me a hard look and then tapped me on the shoulder. 'Bloody good decision,' he said, and he never mentioned it again.

The only time I have known the Duke to shirk his responsibilities on the cricket field was an occasion when I would probably have done the same myself. We were playing the Allied Breweries team at Burton-on-Trent, a lovely ground with a really superb wicket. We noticed when we arrived that one of their players was A. Ward, who turned out to be the former Derbyshire and England fast bowler Alan Ward. Needless to say, this discovery set quite a few pulses racing.

The Breweries' team batted first and scored around 180, which we would have regarded as quite a reasonable target, had Mr Ward not been playing. Our opening pair went in with knees knocking, and sure enough we had soon lost some early wickets. Then Alan Ward was taken off, partly I think to make sure that the game lasted until the pubs opened. Our middle order batsmen started to score a few, until it began to look as if we could win the game.

At this stage the Breweries' captain brought Ward back into the attack to knock off the remaining wickets. I was down to bat at number eleven, with the Duke at number ten. Our number nine batsman was out to the first ball of an Alan Ward over, and the Duke turned to me and said 'Go on then.'

'I'm not in now,' I said. 'You are. I'm number eleven today.'

'Who's the bloody captain of this team?' he roared.

I could see that there was no alternative but to go out to bat.

I took guard — not that it would have done me much good but it helped to ease the nerves a bit — and waited for Alan Ward to come in off what seemed to be an incredibly long run. I don't mind admitting that I was frightened. I kept telling myself, whatever you do, keep your eye on the ball. In the split second in which I had to make the decision I realised that the ball was pitching on off stump, so I stuck my bat out towards point and my body out towards square leg — you could have driven a tank through the gap — and shut my eyes. The ball caught the edge of the bat and went through the slips at high speed. Four runs.

Guffaws from the boundary indicated that my team-mates were enjoying this, but I certainly wasn't. A fierce look from Alan Ward, when he finally pulled up at the end of his follow-through, indicated that he was not best pleased either. He went back to his mark. Crikey, I thought, I've never been as far as that on my holidays! I

93

concentrated once again on keeping my eye on the ball. This time it was on the leg stump. I managed to get a nick on it, and it flew to the fine leg boundary for another four runs. More laughter from the edge of the field and another furious look from Mr Ward.

The third ball pitched on middle stump and by then my only concern was self-preservation. Instead of trying to get a bat on it, I just turned round and it struck me a painful blow on the backside. There was a loud appeal for LBW, which was turned down, and great merriment from the boundary. By then I was getting a bit annoyed with my colleagues who seemed to be really enjoying my discomfort. The fifth ball sent my middle stump flying, and I have never been so relieved to get out in a cricket match. That over was one of the most terrifying experiences of my life, but I was glad to see the smile wiped off the Duke's face as he had to come in to face the last ball. Somehow he negotiated it, and in the end we actually won the game, but I'd rather have to jump Becher's Brook a dozen times than face Alan Ward again.

★   ★   ★

One of the highlights of our cricket season used to be the Isle of Wight tour, which sadly stopped in the early 1970s when I think we had run out of hotels who would take us! We used to get up to all sorts of high jinks in between cricket matches on that tour, usually quite harmless but occasionally a bit inconvenient to the locals, such as the time when Jeff King and I stuck a rowing boat on the top of a telephone box on the way home from the pub one night. The next morning quite a crowd had gathered round the boat, scratching their heads in bewilderment, so Kingy stuck his head out of the hotel window across the road.

'Bloody hell!' he shouted. 'Must have been a bloody high tide last night!'

One year Jeff brought his wife with him. This sort of

thing wasn't encouraged, but as their first wedding anniversary occurred during the tour I think Maureen had made it clear that Jeff only went if she came too. In the evenings most of us would stay up quite late playing cards and having a few drinks, so when Jeff and Maureen announced that they were going off to bed before midnight they got a pretty ribald reception. Now in those days we used to stay in two hotels which were more or less next door to each other, and Jeff and Maureen had to leave our hotel to go to their own, so a group of us decided to accompany them to their room. Maureen finally kicked us all out, but not before Terry Biddlecombe had pinched a pair of her pyjamas. They were 'baby doll' pyjamas, very sexy, and Terry changed into them before we left the hotel. Then he minced along the pavement to our own hotel wishing all the passers-by 'Good evening'. There were some very shocked faces and it's a wonder no one called the police!

On one occasion when we played cards long into the night, we ran out of champagne. So the next time I went to the gents I took an empty bottle with me and peed into it, then I put it back by the card table and waited to see who would take the bait. A little later Macer Gifford came in after a good night out. 'Ah!' he said, spying the bottle. 'Champagne.' I thought we had our first customer but Macer suddenly realised how strange it was that here was a half-full bottle of bubbly and no one drinking. He smelt a rat, or he might even have smelt something else, and he went off to bed.

Those of us in the card school stayed up all night. At about eight o'clock the following morning Gerald Dartnell came down fresh as a daisy. 'Oh good, champagne,' he said, and lifted the bottle to his lips. It all happened too quickly for us to stop him, and if there is such a colour as bright white that is the shade that Gerald went when he tasted the contents of the bottle!

I think most of the hotels on the Isle of Wight must have got fed up with our antics because we arrived there one year to find ourselves staying in a Pontins holiday camp. This wasn't too bad because we were out all day playing cricket and all evening socialising, but when we *were* there we were usually in trouble because holiday camps are run like boarding schools — you have to obey the rules.

We arrived back at the camp quite late one evening after visiting a few local hostelries and some wag suggested a late-night game of cricket. The chalets were arranged in squares with a lawn in the middle, so we marked out a wicket and the game started. The only light came from some rather dim bulbs hung on the chalet fronts around the square. That year Richard Rumble was with us. Butch, as he was known, acted as the team's secretary and treasurer for years. He didn't play much but he liked to come on the tours when he could. Anyway, someone hit the ball straight back past the bowler and it disappeared between two chalets, so Butch went in pursuit. After a while he still had not returned and we thought he must be having trouble finding the ball, so a few of us went to help him. We found Butch lying flat out between the two chalets with a bloody great lump on his forehead. Someone had left a chalet window open and in the darkness Butch had cannoned straight into it!

The next morning we were late for breakfast, which was frowned upon, so David Nicholson was hauled up in front of the camp 'commandant' and given a lecture about being late for meals and making a noise in the chalet area at night. Our captain duly promised there would be no more midnight cricket matches, so when we came back the following evening we had to think of something else to amuse ourselves. We ending up parachuting with umbrellas off the high diving board into the swimming pool, but this only resulted in another bollocking from the CO, and we never stayed at Pontins again!

My brother Tom was with us on that tour, and being a virtual teetotaller he didn't altogether approve of the amount of boozing and larking about that went on. Before the parachuting escapade started he had demanded that we

Evenings on cricket tours consisted of many varied forms of entertainment. Here the Duke (David Nicholson), on the far right, has just dropped the flag to start the hobby-horse race. From left: myself making the running; Josh Gifford; Terry Biddlecombe interfering with Josh; David McCreary interfering with Terry; Jeff King going out of the side door; Macer Gifford displaying a good crouch; Andy Turnell riding as short as ever; and Jack Cook, who won the 1971 National on Specify.

stop every so often for a head-count, because he didn't want to find anyone lying in a drunken stupor in twelve feet of water. After about twenty minutes he called for the first count-up. There were twelve of us altogether, and Jeff King and I hid in some bushes. Tom, however, still managed to count up to twelve, and then gave everyone permission to carry on fooling about. Considering he was

stone-cold sober, I hate to think what figure he would have arrived at if he'd had a few drinks!

Macer Gifford played a lot of cricket for the jockeys' team. He was a great competitor, a very funny man and a good friend, and it was tragic that he died so young of motor neurone disease. When he was fielding and the ball came his way he would get down in the classic coaching manual style, hands and knees behind the ball, but at the last minute he would jump up again and the ball would clatter him on the shins. Quite often the batsmen got an extra run as Macer hopped about in agony! Eventually he took to wearing football shinpads. In the slips too he was always technically perfect, crouched down, hands in front of him, eye on the angle of the bat waiting for a deflected catch. I was standing next to him one day when I was sure the batsman was going to snick it to us, but he got his bat out of the way at the last second.

'I thought we were going to get one there, Macer,' I said.

'So did I,' he replied. 'I was just getting ready to duck!'

I once hitched a lift with him to a game, and he was stopped for speeding in Devizes.

'Do you realise, sir,' the policeman said, 'that you were travelling at forty-six miles per hour in an area where the speed limit is thirty miles per hour?'

Macer shook his head sadly. 'Dear oh dear,' he said. 'Forty-six miles per hour. I just can't understand it, officer, I wasn't in a hurry!'

It was just as well that there was no breathalyser in those days or quite a few of us would have been in trouble on the way back from cricket matches. Fortunately, on the Isle of Wight tours we travelled by coach.

One day, after a game at Cowes, we had a few beers

The Duke has just won the knobbly knees contest. Macer Gifford is trying to unseat him, while Victor Dartnell and I offer support. It says much for the camaraderie of jump racing that we spent so much time in each others' company during the off-season.

A spot of clay pigeon shooting in between games of cricket. From left: Tim Norman, Terry Biddlecombe, myself, our host, Richard Tate, David Nicholson, Jeff King and Josh Gifford. Kingy has already swapped his gun for a more long-term form of self-destruction.

with the opposition before boarding the coach which would take us back to our hotel in Sandown, which is more or less at the opposite side of the island. It became obvious that our coach driver was pretty useless when we passed the ground again half an hour after we had left it! By this time the beer was doing its work and quite a few of us needed the loo. We asked the coach driver to stop, but he didn't appear to hear us, and when he finally did hear us he said he couldn't stop anyway. Things were getting desperate, but Jeff King came to the rescue in his usual forthright way. He got out of his seat and stood next to the driver, then he pulled his trousers down.

'If you don't stop this bloody coach right now,' he threatened. 'I'm going to piss down your back!'

I've never seen a coach stop so suddenly, or empty so quickly.

★ ★ ★

The jockeys' cricket team colours are buff and gold, the racing colours of the Queen Mother, who was the team's patron. One day, when we were playing near Ascot, we got word that the Queen Mother was coming over, and at the appointed hour David Nicholson had both teams lined up ready to be presented to Her Majesty. She was absolutely charming and spoke to each person individually. I remember that she asked me how Foinavon was getting on.

A few years later the Queen Mother was due to visit Mr Courage's yard. My wife's grandmother was staying with us at the time so I took her over to Edgcote and installed her in the tackroom where she would have a good view from the window as the Queen Mother went past. When Her Majesty arrived at the yard Mr Courage saw me peering through the window and called me out to be introduced.

'Oh!' she said. 'I've met you before. It was at a cricket match at Ascot.'

I could only marvel at her memory, and think how lucky we were to have such a charming patron.

8

MORE TALES FROM THE WEIGHING ROOM

I have not missed a Grand National meeting for twenty years now, as jockey or valet, and I hope I've got a few more to look forward to, because the weighing room on Grand National day has an atmosphere all of its own. There is no other racing day to beat it, not even the Cheltenham Gold Cup. It is unique.

My preparations for Aintree start quite a few weeks before the meeting itself. Once the Cheltenham Festival meeting is over, jockeys with Grand National rides start thinking about Liverpool, and I hear frequent cries of 'Hey, Buck, make sure my tack's spot-on for Liverpool, won't you?' Some trainers say the same thing too — I remember Jenny Pitman asking me to make doubly sure about Ben de Haan's tack the year he won on Corbiere. It goes without saying that I will always ensure that everyone's tack is dead right, but I don't mind trainers asking me: they prepare the horses, I make ready the tack just as carefully. Some jockeys, like Simon Sherwood, are more laid back and don't seem to worry about it, but I ask every jockey what he's riding in the National and which saddle he will need. If a saddle broke I would feel partly responsible. A few years ago Hywel Davies was riding Royal Stuart and was going well when he fell at the fence before Becher's second time round. We were watching it on television in the weighing room and someone said 'His leather's snapped.' I felt terrible until he came back in and I realised they were a brand new pair of leathers which he had bought especially for the race.

Aintree is unique for a number of reasons. The Grand National is quite simply the world's greatest steeplechase, and, as such, people all over the world who follow jump racing know about it, whereas a lot of them have never heard of the Gold Cup. The National is shown live in Australia, at two o'clock in the morning. When Hywel Davies went to ride in Australia a couple of months after Last Suspect's win, the media there had no need to comment on his background and his record as a jockey. He had won the National, and that was enough. The race has history, tradition, charisma, frightening fences, money, tragedy and triumph on a grand scale. Nothing else will ever beat it.

For me, nowadays, the Liverpool meeting starts at six o'clock on the Thursday morning when I leave home to drive up to Aintree with Andrew Townsend. I always stay in the same digs, Mrs Summerfield's opposite the race-course, and I wouldn't go anywhere else. I'm on the course by ten o'clock that morning. The first two days are more or less like a normal meeting, although you can feel the tension gradually building up.

On Grand National day itself I'm in the weighing room by nine o'clock, which gives me plenty of time to double-check everyone's tack. On a normal race day jockeys wouldn't be there until an hour before the first race, but on the big day some of them will have been riding work out on the course so they'll stick their heads in early. I will have done as much as possible on the Friday night — polishing boots and so on — so that on Saturday morning I can concentrate on any last-minute details as well as deal with all the requests and reminders from jockeys, trainers and head lads, which seem to double in quantity on National day.

As the race itself draws near, the atmosphere gets very tense and things become more and more hectic. It is quite a job to get all the correct saddles, colours and weights ready for forty runners, especially as some of them will have ridden in the previous race. They have to weigh in from that and then weigh out again in time for the parade. I try to keep an eye on the less experienced ones to make sure they don't get too tensed up. The jokes and wisecracks come faster than ever as everyone attempts to stave off the nerves, although some jockeys, like Richard Dunwoody in 1986, manage to stay very cool.

Once they're out of the weighing room there's nothing more I can do, so Andrew and I get on with preparing for the next race and watch the National itself on television. I am always concerned about fallers, and so are the other jockeys when they come back in. The atmosphere then is quite different — the tension has gone, everyone is talking about how their own race went, watching the replay on the television and laughing and joking about it all. There is no bitterness or envy from jockeys who have seen their chances come to nothing due to a fall or being beaten by an outsider. Everyone is just glad it's over, and glad that they're still in one piece.

Whenever one of my jockeys gets hurt I always go to the ambulance room to make sure he's all right. Sometimes, if he isn't, I have to arrange to get messages to the wife or for his car to be got home. I remember a young kid at Wincanton who broke his leg so badly that it was bent in half and the bone had gone through his boot. You could pour the blood out of the boot afterwards. A pair of boots costs £70 so I pull them off whenever possible, always with a doctor present and the nurse gently holding the leg down. When Bugsy Hughes was badly hurt at Towcester I was called in to pull his boots off, but he looked to me as though he was in a very bad way, so I said 'Leave him, just let him breathe.' I think I made the right decision because it turned out that he had a punctured lung, broken ribs and a caved-in chest bone.

Steve Smith Eccles called me into the ambulance room once when he had a suspected fractured leg. John Francome was there too and he hated to see anyone injured. He asked me to cut Steve's boots off but Steve said 'No, you won't cut the bloody things off. Buck'll pull them off.'

'I'll buy you a new pair if you're afraid of paying for them yourself,' John said. But Steve wasn't having it.

'No,' he said. 'Buck'll pull them off.' And I did. Fortunately he wasn't as badly hurt as we feared.

I remember another time when Steve got hurt, not on the track but in the weighing room, and he swears it was all my fault. In a way I suppose it was. It was one of those rare occasions when two jockeys were arguing and the whole thing looked like developing into fisticuffs. If this ever happens I try to defuse the situation as quickly as possible because there would be hell to pay if the stewards found out.

Steve came into the weighing room at Warwick arguing with Billy Morris about something that had happened on the course. Both were saying it was the other's fault, when suddenly Steve went for Billy. I was right behind Steve so I grabbed him by the shoulders and held his arms back, thinking that would stop it. But Billy took a swing anyway and hit the defenceless Steve straight in the eye. His eye came up like a golf ball and he was furious. He went on at me for weeks about it.

'Where did you get that black eye, Eck?' people would ask him.

'Ask that silly bugger!' he would reply, jerking his thumb in my direction.

I remember another incident in the weighing room at Hereford, when Bob Wooley, who was a big chap for a jockey, came in cursing and muttering.

'Who was that little sod on my outside coming into the straight?' he asked in a loud voice.

'That was Johnny Williams,' someone answered. Johnny only weighs about eight stone wringing wet.

'Good job it was him,' growled Bob Wooley. 'Because

if it had been anyone bigger I'd have given him a bloody good hiding.'

Just for the hell of it, I said 'Hang on Bob. I wouldn't take on Johnny Williams if I were you. He's a tough little bugger.'

Bob wasn't impressed. 'I wasn't ABA champion for nothing,' he said.

'Never mind that,' I said, really stirring things up now. 'Johnny will still give you a damn good hiding.'

At that point in came Johnny himself, struggling as usual with a big saddle and a bagful of lead. Bob grabbed him and butted him. Johnny threw down his saddle and went for Bob like a terrier, so my brother and I grabbed one each and pulled them apart, kicking furiously. It had looked a bit like David taking on Goliath. But these things never last long. The following day I saw Bob and Johnny sitting on the bench chatting happily to each other.

★   ★   ★

Another role that I play in the weighing room is that of father confessor, whether it is looking after a new young jockey or giving advice to a more experienced one. I remember Jenny Pitman once sent a little kid to me to be fitted up with breeches and boots, and asked me to keep an eye on him. He was a tiny little chap with legs like matchsticks and size nine feet, which looked a bit out of proportion. We had to pad his boots up with shinguards to stop his legs rattling around inside them. Anyway, that youngster turned out to be Brendan Powell, and he hasn't done too badly for himself since then!

I give jockeys whatever advice I can, whether it's how to ride a certain course or what to say if they've been called up by the stewards. I suppose they come to me because

On a hot racing day in early autumn I share an ice-cream with Steve Smith Eccles on the weighing room steps.

I'm older and more experienced than they are, but at the same time they can identify more with me than they can with a trainer or a racecourse official.

Once, an up-and-coming young jockey approached me for advice about a job offer. At the time he was with a middle-of-the-road trainer, and he had been offered a much better job with a top trainer, which would have certainly meant a better retainer and more winners. He asked me what he should do, because he didn't want to upset anyone.

I said 'Don't go to your guv'nor and say "I'm leaving to go to so-and-so's yard." Go to him and say "Can you give me a bit of advice," and then explain the position. When he sees it that way he'll understand.'

The jockey in question acted on my advice, but unfortunately his guv'nor did not react as predicted and instead told him he would be an idiot to move. So the jockey had to say 'Thanks for your advice but I'm going anyway.' His guv'nor was not best pleased, but the lad himself certainly did the right thing: he's not looked back ever since and is now one of the country's leading jump jockeys.

9

HEROES AND CONTEMPORARIES

'Oi!' The forefinger was pointed at my chest in a familiar stabbing motion. 'I want you at my place on Wednesday morning, ten o'clock sharp!'

The forefinger belonged to David Nicholson, and, of course, it didn't matter to him what I might be planning to do or where I might be going that day. It could have been Plumpton in which case I would be miles away from Condicote by ten o'clock, but as it happened I was due at Worcester so I knew I could arrange for my brother to go on ahead of me.

'Bring some decent breeches and boots to fit a woman,' David ordered.

'What sort of woman?' I asked him.

'Can't tell you that.'

'Well that's a lot of good, David,' I said. 'I must have some idea.'

He gave me one of his long hard looks and said 'Strictly between you and me and no one else, I want you to fit Princess Anne.'

Well, at least I knew what I had to do. I sorted out some of the best stuff from all the equipment I keep at home and on the appointed day I set off for Condicote in plenty of time. Now, I've been driving BMWs for a long time —

I'm on my fifth at the moment — and I have never had a moment's trouble with them, except on that particular day, of all days! I hadn't been driving very long when the oil light started flashing and I knew something was wrong. I pulled into a garage and it transpired that there was a leak which would have to be repaired before I could go on. I was wondering how I was going to get out of this mess, when by pure chance the next person to drive into the garage forecourt was my brother's brother-in-law, David Morris.

'You're looking a bit flustered, Buck,' he said.

I explained that it was vitally important for me to be at Condicote by ten o'clock, although I didn't tell him why. I had kept my word to David and told no one except my wife Ann. Fortunately he was able to help and, by borrowing Tom's wife's car, I arrived at the Duke's yard only a couple of minutes late. Princess Anne was already there, drinking coffee in the Nicholson's kitchen, and if you didn't know who she was she could have been just another member of the household.

The boots I gave her to try were spot-on, and she was delighted. They had been made for Graham McCourt but were slightly too small for him. 'You're bloody magic you are,' said the Duke. And I thought, crikey, that's a compliment coming from him. The breeches were fine too, but the Duke was not entirely satisfied.

'Wrong material,' he said. 'Get some of that stuff we used to ride in.'

'Where the hell am I going to get that stuff?' I said. Jockeys hadn't used it in years.

The Duke was not to be put off. 'We don't want any of this nylon stuff,' he said. 'Get some of that decent material Goldings used to make.'

I wasn't able to find any of it, but in the end I did get hold of some suitable material. I had the breeches made up and gave them to the Duke to pass on to Princess Anne.

I met the Princess again a few months later when she presented all the surviving Grand National winners with a

During the 1985 Grand National meeting all the surviving National-winning jockeys were presented with a commemorative vase by Princess Anne. She is about to pass comment on the boots for which I had fitted her a few weeks earlier.

trophy during the 1985 Aintree meeting. She remarked then how well the boots fitted, but said that the breeches were slightly too big, so I promised to have another pair made. The Princess was smashing and very charming, and the trophy she presented to me that day will always be one of my most prized possessions.

Life as a jockeys' valet sometimes seems mundane, but meeting people like Princess Anne and the Queen Mother certainly makes up for the more routine times and there have been many highlights during my life in racing which have made all the hard work worthwhile.

★ ★ ★

Most young lads have a hero and I was no exception. My hero was Fred Winter and I absolutely idolised him. Fred was in his prime as a jockey when I was new to the game, and if you asked me now who I rated best between him and John Francome I honestly could not split them. They both had similar riding styles, and as far as I'm concerned no one else I've ever seen riding can touch them. I would also rate Fred as a brilliant trainer.

I rode against Fred Winter in a three-mile chase one foggy day at Wolverhampton. He was champion jockey then and I was still a claimer. I was riding one of the Courage horses, a mare called Lira, and Fred was on a horse called Vultrix.

It soon developed into a two-horse race and we were out on our own with two whole circuits to go. On the far side of the course there were a couple of chaps employed to step in the sods of turf that the horses hooves cut up, and in the fog we didn't see them until the last minute. There was no time to shout a warning and we just flew either side of them, which I imagine gave them something to think about! We came over the last fence neck and neck, but then Fred's vast experience and brilliant finishing told, and he beat me on the run-in by a short head. As we pulled

The great John Francome in action, showing the style which made him Champion Jockey seven times. Here he is (TOP) at Newbury in November 1975 — the first season he won the Championship — and (BOTTOM) leading the field on Brown Chamberlain during the 1984 Cheltenham Gold Cup. Despite all John's work at the finish, he was beaten on the run-in by Phil Tuck on that superb chaser Burrough Hill Lad (far left, striped sleeves).

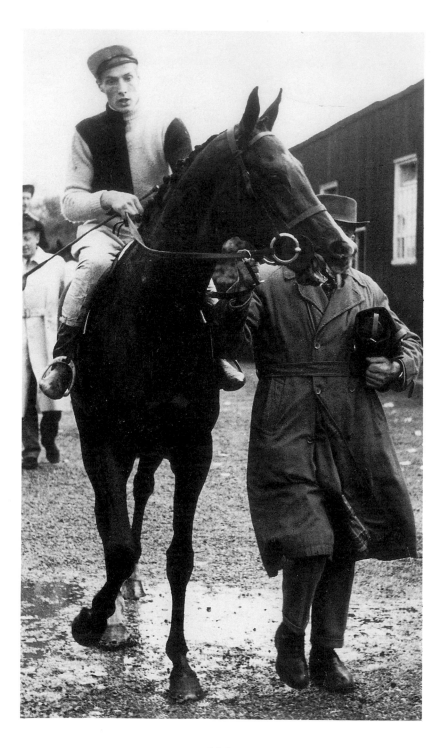

114

up together he said to me, 'Do you know, if every race I'd won had been as hard as that I'd have packed up years ago.' I was really thrilled by what he said and by the exciting ride I'd just had, and I came back to unsaddle feeling just as pleased as if I'd won the race.

Lira was a game little mare and I had some other good rides on her. At Sandown once, she had been entered in a three-and-a-half-mile chase in which the mighty Arkle was also a runner. We left Lira in at the overnight stage in case the race cut up. During the race she and I went all the way round upsides Arkle until we got to the Pond fence on the final circuit. After we jumped that the great horse just went up a gear and was gone, making the rest of the field look one-paced and illustrating why he was in a class of his own. It was a great moment nevertheless, and in the weighing room afterwards Pat Taaffe remarked what a good little jumper Lira was.

Lira also shared with me an experience which I think is probably unique in racing. It was a three-mile chase at Market Rasen. She'd won there before over the same distance and I fancied my chances.

After the start at Market Rasen you jump a plain fence followed by a ditch, and next to this ditch is another plain fence which you jump as you set out on the final circuit. So, after one circuit we jumped the first again and the other nine horses jumped the ditch, but I jumped the plain fence on my own. All the other jockeys told me I'd gone wrong and that I might as well pull up there and then, but I knew I was right. We completed the final circuit, jumped the last and pulled up. I finished second to a horse ridden by George Lee.

Now the distance from the racecourse to the unsaddling enclosure at Market Rasen is a long one — about 400 yards

Lira, the game little mare who gave me many a good ride, including an unforgettable experience upsides Arkle all the way round Sandown, until the great horse changed gear at the second last and forged ahead with ease.

115

— and Mrs Courage was waiting at the edge of the course. She gave me a tremendous bollocking all the way up to the unsaddling enclosure, much to George Lee's amusement. It was an uncomfortable experience but I was convinced I had done the right thing.

'Well, nine other jockeys can't be wrong,' said Mrs Courage.

'I think they are,' I replied quietly.

As soon as I had weighed in, I objected to the winner. This took the stewards rather by surprise and they even went out on to the course to look at the fence, but in the end it turned out that I had done the right thing. The stewards disqualified all the other nine runners, which wiped the smile off George Lee's face, and Mrs Courage took all the place money as well. She didn't say much to me about it, but I had a good laugh listening to the reports on the radio on the way home.

As a jockey, Market Rasen was always one of my favourite courses, along with Sandown and Cheltenham, and I liked Towcester too. The Courage horses always ran well at Towcester, probably because the course was very similar to our gallops. For some reason or other I hated Fontwell and Southwell, and Windsor was often a difficult course because it gets so wet when the river floods. I also used to enjoy the courses in the South-west — Devon and Exeter, Newton Abbot and Taunton. When I was riding, the trip to the West Country could take up to seven hours in holiday traffic, because there were no motorways then, so we used to take two or three horses and stay down there for a fortnight, which was good fun at the start of the season when the weather was still good.

Stan Mellor was one of my riding contemporaries, but like Fred Winter he was a little senior to me in terms of age and experience. That seniority was illustrated in a very annoying manner at Stratford once, when I was riding a horse called Doornob in a chase. We came to the last upsides Stan's horse and well in front of the rest of the field, when Stan's horse gave us a helluva bump. We ended up on the hurdle track but I managed to get back at him and he only won by half a length. As I was unsaddling I told the trainer, Ray Peacock, what had happened and said to him that I reckoned we could get the race on an objection. So, after I weighed in, I objected to Stan's horse for bumping and taking my ground. I was called into the stewards' room and I stood to attention — as we did in those days — waiting for Stan to appear. When he came in one of the stewards stood up and said 'Hello Stanley, well done!' Bloody hell, I thought, what am I doing here? I've got no chance. Sure enough they sent me out with a flea in my ear and I was very annoyed about the whole episode.

Fortunately my encounters with the stewards never assumed Francome-like proportions, and I recall only one other instance when I reckoned I was hard done-by. It was after a four-year-old novice hurdle at Ascot in which I was riding Pride of Kentucky for Mr Courage. There were thirty-odd runners in the race and I was involved in a blanket finish with five or six other horses for fourth place. It was obviously going to take some time for the judges to sort out the photo so we unsaddled in the unsaddling area and went to weigh in, and it was only then that I learned that it was I who was fourth. A few minutes later I was called into the stewards' room.

'Do you realise you were fourth?' someone asked.

'Yes sir.'

'Do you know that there is a fourth place enclosure?'

'Yes sir.'

'Well why didn't you go into it?'

I explained that, because there was a photo between half a dozen horses, we couldn't all go into the fourth enclosure and also that we couldn't all stay on the horses' backs while they sorted out the photo, so we had all dismounted in the unsaddling area outside the ring.

The stewards listened to all this and then asked me to wait outside. After a while they called me back in and told me they were fining me £35 for not going into the fourth enclosure.

I was bloody furious! I felt like asking them if they thought I was capable of sorting out the photo before it was even developed; and in any case the whole thing was an extremely trivial matter. Also, in those days thirty-five quid was worth a good deal more than it is now! I made a mental note not to get on the wrong side of the Ascot stewards in future.

Ron Atkins, one of the jockeys who turned down the Grand National ride on Foinavon because he didn't think the money was right, also had a nasty experience at Ascot. He was riding in a novice chase and he fell going down the hill towards Swinley Bottom. He wasn't hurt, so he hitched a lift in a course car which was carrying Bill Smith, who had fallen too. There were quite a lot of fallers in this particular race and I think only four horses finished out of a field of fourteen.

The car dropped them by the finishing post on the inside of the course, so Ron and Bill started to walk across the course to get back to the weighing room. The race had finished and they were chatting away when suddenly a loose horse came galloping out of the gloom and knocked Ron senseless. He woke up in hospital surrounded by some of the other jockeys who had fallen, but the irony of the whole episode was that the horse that had knocked him out was the one he had been riding in the race!

Another contemporary of mine who nearly got into very serious trouble with the stewards, but in fact got out of it in a clever way, was Johnny Gamble — in this case appropriately named.

It is strictly against the rules of racing for jockeys to bet (the same applies to valets incidentally). Anyway, Johnny ignored this at Newbury one day and went into the ring to have a punt. As he was walking away, he noticed one of the stewards nearby, and wondered if the fellow had seen him placing his bet. Sure enough, soon afterwards, the public address system asked for the jockey Johnny Gamble to report to the stewards' room after the second race.

Johnny was wearing a dark suit and a trilby. He also,

A study in concentration from Ron Atkins and myself at Newton Abbot in August 1966. I very rarely wore goggles when I rode.

luckily, lived in Newbury. He ran to the main gate, grabbed a taxi, and directed it to his house. When he got there he told the driver to keep the meter running while he dashed inside and swapped his suit for flannels and sports jacket and his trilby for a flat cap. Then he rushed back to the racecourse. He reported to the stewards' room as instructed, and the man who had spotted him in the ring looked at him with some surprise, muttered 'Sorry, there's been a mistake', and let him go!

One of the nicest people I have ever encountered in racing was Tim Brookshaw. I was sitting alone in the weighing room at Wolverhampton once, during my first season when I hardly knew anyone. Tim, who had never met me before, came over and put his arm round me and said 'Cheer up son, it may never happen!' Tim was second in the 1959 National on Wynburgh, behind Michael Scudamore on Oxo, and he was also champion jockey in the 1958/9 season. But then he had a terrible fall in a hurdle race at Liverpool when his horse ducked out and went through the rails. He was told that he would never walk again, but he not only walked, he rode.

It was at Finmere show, which a lot of jockeys used to attend to raise money for Stoke Mandeville hospital. We rode the show jumping course which was no pushover since it was a qualifier for Wembley. Tim had jumped three parts of the way round when he came to a double. As a result of his accident he couldn't kick with his legs, but he used his hands well and really sent the horse into it. Unfortunately, he stood right off at the first, landed short, took off too early for the second and went out the side door. We rushed over to pick him up, and a groom began to lead the horse away, but Tim wasn't finished.

'Bring that bloody animal back here!' he roared. And he insisted on us putting him back on it. The crowd went mad.

Tim Brookshaw is dead now, but in his time he was a very brave man and a thoroughly good jockey who rode a lot of winners. Everybody loved him.

Another great character from those days was Mick Batchelor. He was a hard man, and a super jockey, and when he retired from race riding he came to live quite near me and used to ride out for the Courage stable occasionally. A couple of days before the 1967 National I saw Mick in our local pub. I told him I'd got the ride on Foinavon and asked him for advice on how to ride in the big race. 'Keep one leg on each side of the bloody horse, and make sure you stay there,' was his reply.

In those days there was a northern champion and a southern champion in jump racing and Mick was northern

Josh Gifford and Terry Biddlecombe at a gymkhana a few years after
they retired. By now Biddles is putting up a few pounds overweight.
On the right is Tim Brookshaw, a very courageous man who was
Champion Jockey in 1958/9 but was later paralysed in a bad fall at
Aintree. As you can see, it didn't stop him from riding.

champion on two or three occasions. Once, when he was
talking about the National, someone asked him if he sat
back at Becher's. 'I don't know about sitting back,' he said.
'But I didn't regain my crouch until I reached the Canal
turn.'

Now that I've reached 'elder statesman' status as a

121

National jockey some of the youngsters ask my advice on how to ride the race. Sometimes I feel like repeating Mick Batchelor's words, but instead I tell them to get between the inner and the middle. I always did and I always had super rides in the race, and Josh Gifford was another one who went that way. I know others prefer the outside, where they reckon there's less chance of getting into trouble, and, you will remember, Hywel Davies steered that course on Last Suspect in 1985, but I reckon it's much longer. I have seen horses going to Becher's on the inner, five lengths behind something on the outer, and yet by the next fence they'll be five lengths in front.

Brian Fletcher always took Red Rum between the inner and middle. I believe that Brian was an extremely good Grand National jockey and anyone who disagrees only needs to look at his record — one third place behind Josh and me in 1967, second on Red Rum in 1975 and three wins, twice on Rummy and once on Red Alligator. I also think, with no disrespect to Tommy Stack, that Brian would have won had he been riding Red Rum in 1976, because he would have kicked on earlier. Brian was very disappointed when he was jocked off Rummy, and he disappeared from the racing scene for a while, so it was good to see him again when we all got our trophies at the 1986 meeting.

Sometimes I have tried to help other jockeys by getting them spare rides, for which they are usually grateful, because one spare ride for a struggling young jockey can lead to good things. Once, when I was still riding myself, there was a spare going in a novice chase at Wolverhampton. 'Jack Berry'll ride it,' I said. And he did. Unfortunately, as I jumped the ditch, I looked down and there was Jack on the floor shaking his fist at me! 'Fancy sticking me in for a bloody awful ride like that!' he said later.

These days, if a jockey is hurt and can't ride in his next race, the trainer will often ask us valets who is available to replace him, and we have certain jockeys that we like to put up. Once, at Sandown, a trainer asked for a jockey and

I put up Vic Soane, who was duly grateful. When he came back in though, he had changed his tune a bit.

'Don't you buggers ever stick me in for a ride like that again!' he said. 'The bloody thing tried to pull up at every hurdle.'

'How do I know how they jump?' I said. 'Perhaps you'd like me to go out and school them first?'

★　★　★

Looking back over the past thirty-odd years I realise that I've had a very satisfying life. I still don't know what made me decide to choose the horses instead of the sheep when I went to work for Mr Courage, but whatever it was, I'm grateful. If I'd chosen the sheep, I'd probably never have set foot on a racecourse. Similarly, if Popham Down hadn't run across that 23rd fence at Liverpool all those years ago I'd be just another ex-jockey who did his time in the saddle and then went on to do something else. Instead, and however much luck was involved, the record books show that the 1967 Grand National was won by J. Buckingham riding Foinavon, and that is something of which I am immensely proud. I have met some wonderful people — owners, trainers and fellow jockeys — and ridden some marvellous horses. There have been a few bad moments — the falls, being jocked off Spanish Steps, and the uncertainty about the future when I realised I would have to pack up riding. But, here again, that was resolved by my fellow professionals and the Jockeys' Association, and it's something that I'm very grateful for, because apart from anything else it meant that I could stay in the game. All in all it has been a wonderful thirty years, and if I was starting again I would not choose anything other than a life in racing.